Nurse In The Glen

by

Donna Rix

Dales Large Print Books
Long Preston, North Yorkshire,
BD23 4ND, England.

British Library Cataloguing in Publication Data.

Rix, Donna
        Nurse in the glen.

        A catalogue record of this book is
        available from the British Library

        ISBN   1-84262-021-5 pbk

First published in Great Britain by Robert Hale Limited, 1979

Copyright © Donna Rix, 1979

Cover illustration © Edgeler by arrangement with Allied Artists

The moral right of the author has been asserted

Published in Large Print 2000 by arrangement with
Robert Hale Limited

Dales Large Print is an imprint of Library Magna Books Ltd.

Printed and bound in Great Britain by
T.J. (International) Ltd., Cornwall, PL28 8RW

ONE

Lorna Parry sighed unconsciously as she entered the small general hospital in the Scottish town of Rossglen, and smiled wryly to herself as she walked along the wide corridor to the Assistant Matron's office, her blue eyes bright and her lovely face set in the firm expression she usually wore on duty. It seemed that she changed character completely whenever she walked through the doorway of the hospital, and that's why she liked duty, because it enabled her to become immersed in other people's problems and to forget her own. Since her husband and four-year-old son had drowned in a boating accident she had found that work was her only salvation.

She forced herself to climb out of the rut of everyday recrimination, although she had been in no way responsible for what had happened two years earlier. But she blamed herself for not having been with them. A powerful swimmer herself, she might have saved them, and it was this feeling of guilt which hurt. But time was healing her scarred mind, albeit very slowly. Now the third anniversary of their death was approaching, and she could remember as if it were only yesterday the terrible afternoon of the tragedy.

'Sister Parry!' The strident voice cut through her thoughts and she turned quickly, firming her lips when she recognised the tall, powerful figure of Jack Foster, one of the surgeons. Ever since Foster had arrived at the hospital two years ago he had tried everything possible to gain Lorna's interest but made no progress, and now it had become habit for him to ask her for a date. She regarded him intently as he approached with long, easy strides. He was too handsome by far, and knew it; as did some of the nurses, to their cost. 'You get earlier day by day,' he complained. 'You are not supposed to be on duty until two.' He glanced at his watch. 'It's a wonder you don't bring your bed and stay twenty-four hours a day.'

'I have to see Assistant Matron,' she replied, using the old terminology of the hospital. She did not like to think of her colleagues as mere numbers, and most of the staff still used the now out-dated names. 'I'm only fifteen minutes early.'

'But you'll be here until ten this evening, and I'm ready to bet that you won't agree to me driving you home afterwards.'

'You'd win if you put money on it,' she agreed, her eyes glinting.

'I wish I knew what makes you tick. And what it is about you that attracts me. There are a lot of girls falling over themselves to share my off-duty hours, and it's ironic that I can't feel serious about anyone but you, who doesn't want to know me.'

'It's nothing personal,' she retorted. 'But perhaps you're not my type, Jack.' She smiled to soften her words, and saw him shake his head seriously.

'It's a criminal waste,' he declared. 'A girl as beautiful as you should have a man around.'

Lorna glanced at her watch and moved impatiently.

'I must go,' she interrupted. 'Was there anything in particular you wanted to see me about?'

Nothing to do with duty, you can bet. He shook his dark head while a faint scowl showed upon his handsome face. 'I don't know why I bother with you after the countless times you've turned me down, but I'm worried about you. I'm talking as a doctor now. I know what you've got on your mind and it's about time that you snapped out of it.'

'Thanks for the advice, but I think I'm winning the battle in my own way.' She tried to maintain a light tone but failed, and the old familiar pain stabbed through her heart with the sharpness of a scalpel.

'I'll come up to your ward when you're on duty. I need to talk to you.' He held up a hand as she began to protest. 'I shan't broach any personal subject, don't worry. There's a patient in Male Surgical who must have special attention. He was involved in a road accident last night.' As he began to turn away, Foster shook his head again. 'I'll see you in thirty minutes.'

She stared after him as he strode along the corridor. She sighed yet again as she tapped at the door of the Assistant Matron's office, entering when she heard Miss Hayter's invitation.

'Good afternoon, Sister.' Miss Hayter, in her late forties, was short and elfin, her dark eyes ageless, but her wrinkled face and greying hair contradicted her general appearance. She glanced down at her littered desk as Lorna responded to her greeting, and picked up a sheet of note-paper, which Lorna recognised instantly as her request for transfer to night duty. 'I thought I'd have a chat with you before passing this through normal channels. Won't you sit down?'

'Thank you!' Lorna sat down and leaned forward in her chair. For a moment there was silence while they regarded each other. Then Miss Hayter glanced away momentarily, seeming reluctant to go on. But drew a deep breath and plunged in.

'This is an unusual request, Sister. Most people dislike night duty but here are you volunteering to do it permanently.'

'That's why I'm volunteering,' Lorna said quietly. 'No one likes night duty much, but as I don't mind it I thought I'd try and take over permanently and relieve the other Sisters of the onus.'

'I appreciate your consideration, and so would your colleagues, but I'm more concerned about your motive.' Miss Hayter looked into Lorna's pale eyes again, and her tone strengthened. 'Don't get me wrong. You're probably the best Sister we have on the staff, and if everyone performed their duty as well as you there would be far fewer problems on our side. But both Matron and I are concerned about you, Sister. You have suffered a great deal during the past three years. Are you quite sure you've got over your grief now? I mean, you're not planning to hide yourself away on permanent night duty, are you?'

Lorna smiled as she shook her head. 'I suppose it must appear like that, but I assure you that I have fully recovered from the tragedy. I never did worry too much about night duty, and some of the other Sisters do have full lives to lead. I'd like to ease some of the pressures upon them.'

'That's extremely thoughtful of you, but I would like you to rethink the matter before taking this step.'

'I could always later apply to return to day duty if I felt I needed the change.'

Miss Hayter nodded but was not convinced. 'I think you are still in a bit of a rut,' she suggested. 'Would you mind if I took the liberty of calling your father and having an informal chat with him?'

'Please do, if you're concerned about my mental attitude.' Lorna smiled. 'But Father is satisfied that I am perfectly normal.'

'I'm concerned about you for your own interests,' Miss Hayter said. 'Will you permit me to hold your application for a few days? It's not really urgent.'

'That will be all right.' Lorna nodded. 'If you like, I'll get my father to call you when it's convenient. You'd probably have great difficulty in contacting him. He's being run off his feet at the moment with an epidemic of 'flu and mumps.'

'Fine. I'll look forward to him calling.' Miss Hayter smiled. She seemed relieved. 'You know, I can never understand why you didn't become a doctor like your father.'

Lorna arose without comment, a tight little smile on her lips. Departing, she told herself that the only reason she hadn't become a doctor was because she and Peter planned to marry young, and while accepting that she would have continued working as a nurse after marriage, she didn't think that as a doctor she could have handled a husband and a general practice. The dull ache always present in the back of her mind seemed to throb more strongly as she went up to Male Surgical.

Reaching the top of the stairs leading to the ward, Lorna heard the echo of small feet clattering on the tiled floor, and frowned as she peered along the corridor towards the doors of the ward. Even as she looked she saw a boy trip awkwardly and fall heavily, and her teeth clicked together at the sound of his forehead striking the tiled floor. Hurrying forward, aware that visitors were not permitted for another thirty minutes at least, she bent over the child, who was about six years old, and lifted him gently. His face was rather thin, and the dominant feature of it was a pair of piercing brown eyes now shimmering with tears.

'That was quite a fall,' Lorna said sympathetically. 'Have you hurt yourself?' She saw a graze upon his left knee, but was more concerned about the bump he had taken on the head. There was already a noticeable swelling, and the knee was exuding tiny droplets of blood. 'Come into my office and I'll make it better. Can you walk?'

'Yes thank you.' He spoke in rather prim tones, but there was a trembling in his voice and Lorna knew he was trying hard not to cry. She experienced a sudden impulse to pull him into her arms, as she would have done her own son, and a prickling sensation irritated the back of her eyes as she fought down emotion.

'What's your name?' Lorna asked as she took his hand and led him into the ward office.

'Simon Kane. I'm six years old. My Daddy is in that ward. His car crashed last night and he hurt his head. Miss Isobel brought me in with her because there's no one to look after me. Miss Isobel is Daddy's secretary.'

'I see.' Lorna smiled as he looked up at her, and she took hold of his hand, tremoring at their contact. Her own dead son would have been about six years old now, if he had lived. She fought against the surge of emotion as they entered the office. 'Get up on that chair over there and I'll attend to your knee.' She fetched a first aid box as the child obeyed, and quickly bathed the knee and applied a strip of plaster over a square of lint. 'There! You're a brave boy, Simon. I expect it hurts a lot, doesn't it?'

'I'm used to bumping myself. It was my fault. I was running along the passage, and Miss Isobel told me not to. I got what I deserved. That's what Mrs Heywood said. She's our housekeeper.'

'And where is your mother?' Lorna asked. 'Isn't she here with you?'

'Mummy died on the moors. She got lost in the mist and they didn't find her for a week.' The boy volunteered the information in matter-of-fact tones, but the words cut through Lorna.

'I'm sorry to hear that.' Lorna hardly knew what to say. Her mind was fishing for information on the family name Kane. With her father the general practitioner in the district, Lorna was accustomed to learning a lot about the cases of local people, and she fancied that she knew that name Kane but could not immediately recall what she had learned about it. For the past three years she had been totally immersed in her own misery.

'I'd better go back into the passage and wait for Miss Isobel,' he said when Lorna had finished treating him.

'Come along then.' Lorna smiled to herself, for he had a quaint way of speaking. 'And I'll tell Miss Isobel what a brave boy you are.'

'No, don't do that.' His tone was suddenly urgent. 'She told me not to run, and if we don't say anything she may not see the plaster.'

They went out into the corridor and Lorna took him to the door of the ward. When she glanced into his small features she saw worry and concern there, and squeezed his hand gently.

'Don't worry about it. You don't have to say you were running. Just say that you tripped. Now, if you'll wait here I'll go in and see what the situation is. Don't wander away. I'll be back in a few moments.'

Simon nodded seriously and leaned against the wall. Lorna smiled reassuringly at him, noting the pathetic air about him, which caused emotion to lump in her throat. Again she was reminded of her own lost son, and firmed her lips as she entered the ward.

Sister Trent, whom Lorna had to relieve, was emerging from one of the small private wards at the far end of the long general ward, and came quickly towards Lorna. The duty nurses were already busy, and Lorna glanced at her watch, aware that time was flitting by.

'Lorna, you're early, as usual,' greeted Margaret Trent. 'We've got four new patients in since I came on duty this morning. Shall we go into the office? I want to get away as quickly as possible. I have some shopping to do before I can go home.'

'Who is Mr Kane, Margaret?'

'He's lucky to be alive! The police were in this morning. I don't know if a charge of drunken driving will arise from this.'

'What about his injuries?' Lorna cut in, thinking of Simon, who was peering into the ward from the doorway.

'Not serious, we think. He's under observation and suffering from concussion. But Mr Foster will be up to talk to you about Mr Kane.'

'I see. But a secretary brought the child in, didn't she?' Lorna explained what had happened when she arrived.

'That poor kid! He's been here on and off for most of the morning. The secretary is with Mr Kane now. Mr Foster gave her permission, so long as the patient isn't unduly disturbed. It seems that there is some important business Mr Kane must settle today, and it was decided that it would be better to risk pushing up his temperature by letting him complete the business rather than take the risk of his frustration boiling over. He's that kind of a patient, Lorna. Obviously accustomed to having his own way in all things.'

'Some people can get special treatment,' Lorna said quietly.

'If they're as rich and influential as Julian Kane they do,' agreed Sister Trent. She placed a hand upon Simon Kane's head, checking the bump on his forehead. 'I warned you not to run in the corridor, Simon, didn't I?' she said in kindly tones.

'I'm sorry,' he replied contritely.

Sister Trent glanced at Lorna as they entered the office. 'I feel sorry for that lad,' she remarked. 'His father is too occupied with business to have any time for him, and his mother is dead.'

'He was telling me about her. Did she die on the moors?'

'Yes. You were away on a course at the time, if I remember correctly. The woman wasn't local. She had no right to go wandering as she did. But someone ought to have warned her. I don't think it was a happy marriage, by all accounts. He was always busy with his work and she wasn't suited to life in a small Scottish town.' Margaret Trent broke off as Simon followed them into the office. She was anxious to get off duty now. 'You'll find the Seriously Ill list on the desk, and the details of the new admissions and the post-operatives. I'll leave you my notes. It'll save you making out your own list. There's nothing to panic about. See you tomorrow afternoon.'

'Off you go then.' Lorna smiled. 'I'll get by without a picture today.' Sister Trent was always in a hurry. She was married and tried to fit in her hospital duties with her married life. Lorna often changed shifts with her to help her colleague through the more awkward days, and they were very close friends.

Sister Trent opened her handbag and produced a bar of chocolate, which she gave to Simon. The boy thanked her and sat down upon a chair in a corner.

'Am I in the way here, Sister?' he demanded innocently. 'Miss Isobel told me to stay quiet.'

'You're not in the way but I must leave you alone for a few minutes. I have to make sure my nurses arrive on time and do their work.'

'I hope you're not making a nuisance of yourself,' interrupted a voice from the doorway, and Lorna looked around to see a tall, slim blonde standing upon the threshold. 'Hello, Sister. Have you relieved Sister Trent?'

'Yes. I'm Sister Parry.' Lorna moved forward as Simon alighted from his chair and went to the door. 'Simon tripped and bumped his head and scraped a knee. I've taken care of it for him.'

'Poor Simon! You're always in the wars!' She ruffled the boy's hair. 'I'm Isobel Garven, Sister, Mr Kane's secretary. You haven't seen Mr Kane yet?'

'No. Mr Foster, the surgeon, will be coming up shortly to see him, and I'll accompany Mr Foster.'

'Thank you for taking care of Simon. I'm sorry I had to bring him along, but his governess is on holiday at the moment and the housekeeper has more than enough to do without Simon. But he's a good lad.'

'I'm sure he is.' Lorna glanced at the boy and smiled. He was watching her.

'Thank you, Sister,' he said, smiling at her. Then he glanced up at the secretary. 'May I see my father before we go?'

'I'm sorry, but he has done too much already,' came the reply. 'I'll bring you back during visiting hours this evening, Simon. Now we're going into town. I have some letters to type, but before I start we'll get some ice cream for you, shall we?'

'All right. But I'd like to see my father. Is he going to be all right? He won't die like my Mummy did, will he? I wouldn't want to be left all alone.'

He was departing with the secretary as he spoke, but his words cut right through Lorna and she held her breath as she fought down the pain which knifed through her breast. Clenching her teeth, she gazed after the two of them. Simon was holding the secretary's hand, talking animatedly, and she could picture her own dead son as he would have been today. Tears tried to spring to her eyes but she was experienced in holding her emotions at bay and forced herself to concentrate, pushing all personal thoughts into the back of her mind. Her blue eyes hardened as she checked through the reports, and she added to the notes Sister Trent had left. She liked to know which of the patients might need her most during her shift, and a few moments spent in fruitful checking now could prevent a panic later.

But she felt a strange compulsion to see Julian Kane, and left the office to enter the ward. Her own nurses had arrived and were busy as Lorna went to the door leading to the three private wards at the far end of the big ward. Opening the door of Julian Kane's room, she peered in at the figure in the bed.

The man was apparently asleep, wearing a scarlet dressing gown over pale blue pyjamas. He was lying on the top of the bed. Black hair showed through the small gaps in the bandage around his head, and his smooth face was pale.

Lorna entered the room and moved to the bedside, thinking of Simon Kane, and sighed heavily as she studied the set face on the pillow. Julian Kane was in his early thirties, handsome and well-to-do, and she was beginning to recall facts that she had heard about him. He was one of her father's patients, and Dr Parry had spoken of the Kane family that lived in Cairn Manor on the outskirts of Rossglen.

The man on the bed groaned and moved uneasily, his eyelids flickering. Lorna shook her head sympathetically. His wife was dead and his son was a lonely child. Was he suffering the loss of his wife as Lorna herself had suffered over the untimely death of her husband and child? She considered that grim possibility as she gazed down at his immobile face. If he was familiar with the dreadful pangs of inconsolable grief then he had her deepest sympathies. She moved still closer, gazing intently at him, and was filled with a sudden rush of information about him as her memory recalled what she had heard.

At that moment Julian Kane opened his eyes and looked up at her, and it was some little time before Lorna realized she was gazing brazenly at him and that he was aware of it.

'Another Sister!' he said in thin tones. 'Are they coming from all over the hospital to stare at me? What am I, some kind of a peepshow?'

Lorna drew back instantly, filled with confusion, and her face turned scarlet at the expression in his voice. At that moment the door opened and Jack Foster appeared, a smile coming to his lips when he saw Lorna. But she wished the floor could open up to swallow her.

TWO

'I object to being used as an object of curiosity, Doctor!' Julian Kane said when he saw Foster. 'Who is this Sister? Am I not entitled to some privacy in here? I'm paying for the room.'

'This is Sister Parry, Mr Kane, and she's just come on duty.' There was a thin note in Foster's voice, and he glanced at Lorna as if to convey by his expression that he was taking her part.

'Then I'll engage a private nurse to take care of me,' Kane said sharply. 'I don't like a stream of strangers passing through. I'm supposed to be resting, and I can't do that under these conditions. What kind of a hospital is this?'

'We'll keep you until tomorrow morning, when I hope to be able to tell you that

27

you've suffered nothing worse than a bad headache. Your X-rays will be ready shortly.' Foster's voice contained a placating tone. He approached the bed, waving a hand at Lorna to indicate that he wished her to leave. Lorna moved thankfully towards the door, still mentally confused.

'Wait a moment, Sister.' There was irritation in Kane's voice. 'I want some information. If you're on duty then spare me a few moments.'

Lorna turned, instinctively aware that he was one of the worst type of patient. There was always a smattering of his kind in every hospital – people for whom the nurses could do nothing right; patients who had no thought for the staff and believed that nurses were either the lowest form of life or not human at all.

'My son was outside earlier. Why wasn't he permitted to see me?'

'Your secretary took him away.' Lorna had a way of treating his type which usually brought home to them the awareness that their manner was wrong, even if it took some time with some of them.

'Is there any reason why he shouldn't be allowed in to see me?'

'I think you should remain as quiet as possible,' interrupted Foster, trying to take the initiative. 'I permitted your secretary to come in because I thought it would settle you all the quicker, but remember that you have had a bad shock, and if we do find anything wrong with you then you'll need all the strength you've got to fight it.'

'Nonsense! I feel as fit as a fiddle.' Kane glared at Lorna as if she were to blame for his being in hospital. 'I do have a slight headache, but I often get those through pressure of work. I'll be out of here to-morrow, and you'll be lucky if I don't make a complaint at the way I'm being treated.'

Lorna was thinking of Simon Kane as she listened to his tirade, and wondered what kind of a home life the boy led, hoping that he was not being brought up in the way that she suspected. She sensed that the child rarely saw his father, and it was obvious from the way Simon had spoken that he was lonely and repressed; probably surrounded by unsympathetic household employees.

'Mr Kane, I'm sure you'll appreciate that you have to remain as quiet as possible,' Foster said severely. 'You are, of course, at liberty to complain. But we are only concerned in getting you back on your feet and sending you out into the world once more.'

'I don't think he would be so petty or so childish as to make a complaint,' snapped Lorna.

Kane glared at her in the silence that followed, and Lorna could see that Simon had inherited his father's good looks. She felt her heart go out to the boy as she awaited the bursting storm. But Kane looked slightly confused by her attack. He sighed heavily. She smiled wryly, and he noted it.

'Do you find my complaints amusing?' he demanded.

'I wasn't even listening to what you were saying,' she retorted, turning towards the door. 'It seems to me there's nothing you really need, Mr Kane, and I do have a number of very sick patients to care for.'

She glanced at Foster as she departed, as if daring him to comment upon her brusqueness, but she had no intention of accepting Julian Kane's bad manners and petulance, even if he was usually accustomed to treating his own staff as if they were slaves. She went through the long ward back to her office and sat down at the desk to take inventory of the situation.

It surprised her to discover that she was inwardly trembling, and a frown came to her face. Something seemed to have happened to her mind from the moment she saw Kane's son. She was aware of it but could not understand the reason for it.

Nurse Russell appeared in the doorway, a harassed expression on her face.

'Sister, Mr Waring is playing up again. I can't take his temperature.'

'All right, leave him to me. I'll be in the ward shortly.' Lorna sighed and dragged her mind back to duty. She was making hard work of getting into her routine today and it was having a strange effect upon her mind.

When she made her round she began to find life coming back to normal, and by the time she had completed her tour Jack Foster was waiting by the office door. He stepped aside for her to enter, then followed her inside.

'What do you make of Julian Kane?' he demanded. 'Bit of a bully, eh?'

'He appears to take everything for granted and he has no manners at all.'

'You certainly pulled him up short.' Foster smiled. 'But then you are good at putting men in their place.'

She glanced sharply at him, found he was grinning, and let her harsh expression fade. She smiled.

'I'm pleased that he is not seriously injured.'

'He should be able to leave us first thing in

32

the morning if all the tests are negative.'

'Do you suspect anything serious?'

'No. But we're going to make sure before we discharge him. You heard how he was threatening to make complaints. However you have him only until the end of your shift. He'll be out by the time you come on tomorrow, so make the best of it. Send in your nurses if he should want anything. I have the feeling that you and he will strike sparks if you come into contact again.'

'What about visitors?' Lorna glanced at her watch. The afternoon visiting period was about to commence. She wondered if she would get permanent night duty as she had requested, and her blue eyes darkened a little while she considered it.

'I don't think it will hurt him to see one or two, but there is no one to visit him, you know. His wife is dead and his son just went off with the secretary. If you can keep him quiet for the remainder of the day then all well and good.'

'I'll certainly leave him well alone,'

retorted Lorna.

'That's it.' Foster grinned. 'Now let's get round to my favourite topic.'

'The answer is no,' she responded automatically, and he tut-tutted and sighed heavily.

'Three years is a long time to remain in mourning.' There was stark brutality in his voice and she winced. But he continued, 'I don't want to add to what you must be feeling, but as a medical man I must insist that you start taking treatment for what happened to you. I think you need skilled help, Lorna, and I'm the man who can supply it.'

'Thank you for your concern but I'm perfectly all right as I am.' She forced a smile but it was stiff and unnatural. Her eyes were shadowed as she looked down at the papers on the desk, and was afraid to meet his speculative gaze.

'All right.' He turned towards the door. 'But I swear that one day you'll come to me begging to be helped, and by that time it might be too late.'

He departed, and she listened to the sound of his footsteps in the corridor. She sighed helplessly as she thought over what he had said.

Did she need help to get out of the rut into which she had slipped? Was it a bad thing to retain golden memories of a beloved family that had been taken away from her? She felt that it was natural to remember. It was only when grief made one turn aside from the world and reject all human contact that it became wrong. But was that what she was trying to do? This desire for permanent night duty might be a subconscious attempt to get out of the world of reality.

A bell rang on the indicator board and she sighed when she looked up and saw that it was Julian Kane's room. It was her intention to send one of the nurses, but she fought down the impulse and walked along the ward with firm determination. She would stand no nonsense from him.

Kane was sitting on the edge of his bed

when she entered, and he looked up at her, his face pale and drawn.

'I've turned dizzy,' he admitted, holding his head between his hands and looking down at the floor.

Lorna went to his side and felt his pulse. It was erratic and fast. She looked intently into his eyes when he glanced up at her.

'I apologise, Sister, for the way I spoke to you! I haven't been myself for months now. Most things have been going wrong for me and this accident was the last straw.'

'It happens like that sometimes,' she agreed. 'Please be quiet now, would you? And get into bed and lie still. I'll call Mr Foster to have a look at you. I think it was most unwise of you to worry about business this morning.'

'A normal person wouldn't have obtained permission to do it, eh?' he demanded weakly as he stretched out on the bed. 'But Julian Kane always gets his own way.' There was a trace of bitterness in his tone. He gazed at her for a moment. 'You've got blue eyes,' he suddenly accused. 'I thought there was something different about you. Your general colouring is dark but you have blue eyes.'

Lorna said nothing as she unfastened his dressing gown and made him take it off. He got into the bed and she tucked him in then smoothed the covers.

'You're Doctor Parry's daughter, aren't you?'

'Yes.' She was surprised, and looked into his eyes to find that he was regarding her intently.

'When do you go off duty?'

'At ten this evening.'

'I'll probably be going home in the morning. Would you ask your father to call upon me on his round tomorrow?'

'Certainly, but you could get one of your servants to telephone the surgery.'

'I want to talk to him about my son's health, not mine,' he said curtly.

'Simon?' Lorna frowned. 'Is something wrong with him?'

'Do you know my son?'

'I met him when I came on duty.' Lorna explained the child's fall, and Kane shook his head, his lips compressed.

'That poor kid doesn't lead much of a life,' he muttered. 'He hardly ever sees me and doesn't know what family life is.'

'Surely the remedy for that is in your own hands.'

He looked up at her with a frown upon his handsome face.

'Yes,' he said softly. 'It is, but I've never even considered it before. I live in a crazy world of high-pressure business. There are never enough hours in the day for me. No matter how hard and long I work, there is always more work piling up. Time is blurred and distorted. It's like getting on a carousel and being unable to get off.'

'Life itself is like that,' retorted Lorna.

He gazed at her for a moment, then nodded slowly. 'You're right, of course. But I don't want to get morbid. This accident must have knocked a bit of sense into me. I think I'm going to pretend that I'm feeling a lot worse than I really am so that I can have some time to spend with my child. He's all I've got left since his mother died on me.'

'You make that sound as if she did it deliberately.' The words slipped out before Lorna could prevent them, and she set her teeth into her bottom lip. 'I'm sorry,' she apologised instantly. 'I shouldn't have said that.'

But he appeared not to have heard her and she moved away from the bedside.

'I'll call Mr Foster so he can examine you,' she said.

'No, don't do that.' His voice was strong again, and he sat up, easing himself until his head rested against the rail. 'There was nothing wrong with me. I rang because I felt the need to talk to you. I liked the look of you when I first saw you.'

'What kind of help do you need? Are you sure you're not delirious from the accident? Shock sometimes affects people that way.'

'I'm perfectly all right. Perhaps for the first

time in my life I'm right.' He glanced at her left hand. 'You're not married.'

'No.' Her tone was curt.

'You must be in your late twenties. It's strange that a girl as lovely as you is still un-attached. No doubt you have a host of male admirers.'

'There's no one.'

'Do you hate men?' His gaze bored at her.

'No.' She smiled wryly.

'Now I'm prying. I apologise.' His tone changed abruptly and he averted his head. 'You'd better get back to your genuine patients. I'll be out of here in the morning if your precious Mr Foster will give me a clean bill of health.'

Lorna turned obediently and left the room, and she was thoughtful as she went about her duties.

Visiting time was always hectic, and this particular afternoon was no exception. A constant stream of people was entering and leaving the ward. Lorna was beset by anxious relatives asking about the condition and progress of the patients, and spent a great deal of time trying to allay their fears. The two nurses on duty were kept busy fetching vases for flowers while they endeavoured to maintain their normal ward work, and Lorna found that she could not concentrate upon her own duties. Ever since she had arrived at the hospital that afternoon she had been troubled by something niggling at her subconscious mind, and it was made worse by the fact that she could not define the problem.

When the last of the visitors departed it was time for the patients' tea, and the nurses were already busy in the kitchen. Lorna brought her reports up to date and then supervised the special diets. She was on hand when Julian Kane received his tea, and stood in the doorway of his room while one of the nurses took care of him. He watched Lorna with an intense gaze.

'Shall I be able to receive a visitor this evening, Sister?' he called as she was about to depart.

'I should think so, if it's not business you want to discuss.'

'I'd like to see my son. I can't imagine what they must have told him has happened to me. I think it would reassure him if he did see me, don't you?'

'Children are not usually permitted in the wards,' Lorna told him.

'They are, at the discretion of the Ward Sister,' he countered. 'You've met Simon. He's old for his tender years, and he won't make a scene if he sees me. Bring him in yourself when he arrives.'

'All right, I'll let him in to see you, but only for a few moments.'

'Would you ring my home and tell them to bring him along about seven?' He seemed ill at ease, and Lorna nodded.

'I'll call presently. He'll be here at seven.'

'My secretary will bring him. She's doubling as governess for a couple of weeks. Tell her you're to bring him in when he arrives.'

'I get very little time to myself when I'm

on duty,' Lorna reproved, aware that he was giving her instructions and she was prepared to obey them despite her earlier decision to remain impervious to his commanding manner.

'All right, don't bother to call for him. Let him spend all night worrying about his father. He hasn't got a mother, or didn't you know that?'

Lorna caught her breath at his words, and, to her consternation, felt tears stinging her eyes. She drew a deep breath and held it for a moment, then exhaled sharply and blinked rapidly to maintain control of her emotions.

'I'm sorry,' he said contritely. 'I shouldn't have said that. I have taken the liberty of asking some questions about you and learned what happened in your life. I'm playing on your sympathies and it's too bad of me. That's big business for you. Hit them where it hurts the most. But you are basically a good person. All nurses must be or they wouldn't do this job. You're not at all like the people usually surrounding me. They're sharp and selfish, all out for what they can get, and I'm heartily sick of the whole crowd.'

'I'll call your home,' said Lorna, and hurried out of the room, closing the door softly. She was breathing heavily as she went back to her office.

When it was time for her thirty-minute break she went along to the canteen and tried to relax, but found her mind wound up and tense. Her hands were trembling as she lifted a coffee cup to her lips. Sister Lyons of Female Medical came and sat at the same table and they chatted for a few moments.

'You've got Julian Kane in your ward, Lorna,' said Aggie Lyons in her mellow Scots brogue, her brown eyes narrowed and calculating.

'Yes, but I think he's being discharged in the morning.'

'My son works on the estate at Cairn Manor. Some of the things he tells us would make your hair curl. That laddie of Kane's has a dreadful life.'

'He's not ill-treated!' Lorna turned cold inside, and there was a picture of Simon's face in her mind.

'No. Nothing like that. But the boy is being reared by a governess and the housekeeper, and the bairn has no friends and doesn't see a bit of pleasure.'

'That's the impression I got when I saw him this afternoon. But I have the feeling that Mr Kane is going to change matters when he goes home. I think the accident has shocked him into some realisation of the situation. It's pulled him up and made him take stock of his life.'

'I hope you're right, Lorna. He's experienced a lot of tragedy. His wife died out on the moors.'

'That's what I heard.' Lorna suppressed a sigh.

'There was quite a scandal about it about two or three years ago.

'I was away from the town then. Exactly what happened?'

'Nobody really knows. There were a lot of stories going the rounds. She was found dead on the moors. It was officially recorded that she'd gone for a walk, was caught in the mist and died of exposure.'

'And what did rumour say?' Lorna asked, certain that there would be a different story.

'That Julian Kane took her out for a walk, waited for the mist to fall, then left her to die. They didn't get along at all. I heard that they argued and fought terribly. She didn't like living in the wilds of Scotland, as she put it, and he wouldn't consider leaving his ancestral seat.'

'I see.' Lorna nodded. She was beginning to understand the reason for Julian Kane's attitude, and why Simon spoke as he did. She realized that she had become interested in the child and wondered if her own deep patterns of grief had caused her to sub-consciously recognise a fellow sufferer.

When she went back on duty she sat in the office and telephoned Cairn Manor. A man replied in a harsh Scots voice and Lorna gave Julian Kane's message.

'I'll tell Miss Garvin,' the man replied.

'And perhaps you'll tell her to see the Ward Sister before going in to Mr Kane,' added Lorna. She sat for a moment to consider after replacing the receiver, then arose and went along to Julian Kane's room.

He was reading a newspaper. The bandage around his head had worked loose and was unwinding. Lorna fixed it for him, then pumped up his pillows with instinctive movements and straightened the bed covers.

'You're like all the nurses,' he commented. 'Whenever a nurse comes near a bed she pulls the pillows and smooths the covers.'

'Force of habit,' said Lorna with a smile.

'That's better.' His tone was suddenly gentle and he sounded human, less of a business machine. 'That's the first time I've seen you smile. You've got a most severe manner when you're on duty. Are you like it when you get away from here?'

'I wouldn't know.'

'What do you do when you're off duty? I'll stick my neck out by saying that you probably rush home and sit down to read all the medical and nursing journals you can lay your hands on.'

'Are you insinuating that I'm a battleaxe of a nurse?' she asked, smiling to take the sting out of her words.

'I thought you were when you first showed your face in here this afternoon. But I've changed my opinion a great deal since then. If you've suffered in your tragedy as I did when my wife died then you have my sympathy. But if you're still suffering after three years then you ought to get your head examined because you ought to have recovered from it by now.'

'Is there any charge for this advice?' she asked.

He shrugged and shook his head, a thin smile upon his lips. 'I don't know what's getting into me,' he retorted. 'I've never interested myself in other people and their problems.'

48

'It does everyone good to be able to sit down now and again to give some thought to themselves and the world about them,' she observed.

'I've always lived with the knowledge that time is money, and neither should be wasted.'

Lorna took her leave and went about her duties, but as the time drew near for Simon Kane to arrive she began to feel pangs of anticipation creeping through her veins. She tried to settle herself in the office to bring the paperwork up to date before the evening visitors arrived, but her brain was teeming with unusual thoughts and she felt nervous and overstrung. But she forced herself to concentrate until a voice spoke in the doorway of the office.

'Please may I see my Daddy?'

Lorna turned around and saw Simon Kane and the secretary standing there, and arose from her seat, smiling as she went forward.

'Certainly. Your Daddy asked to see you.'

Lorna looked at the secretary. 'Mr Kane would like to see him alone, if you wouldn't mind.'

'That's all right. May I leave him here for an hour and come back later to pick him up?'

'Certainly. That will be all right. I'll keep an eye on him until you return.' Lorna smiled and held out a hand, which Simon took, and she led him through the large ward and into his father's room.

'Daddy!' There was a world of relief in the boy's voice as he ran across the room and jumped upon the bed.

Lorna smiled, but Kane gazed at her as she turned to depart. His eyes were bright, his lips compressed into a thin line.

'Simon can stay for an hour if he doesn't disturb you too much,' Lorna said quietly.

'Do you have to go?' he demanded. 'I want to talk to Simon, but not alone.' He paused and looked down at the boy, who was gazing worriedly at the bandage around his head. 'What I mean is, I don't want to say the wrong things. I want to tell him that the way we've been living is going to change.'

Lorna glanced at her watch, then entered the room and closed the door. 'I have a few moments to spare before the visitors start arriving,' she said, walking to the foot of the bed.

'Did you hurt your head badly, Daddy?' demanded Simon. 'Mrs Heywood said you must have been driving too fast.' He glanced at Lorna. 'My Daddy doesn't do anything wrong,' he added.

'I've got the feeling that I've been doing a lot of wrong things, Simon,' Kane replied seriously. 'I've left you on your own lately, and you haven't had much of a home life. I think we ought to ask someone like Sister Parry, who is an expert in this sort of thing, just what we ought to do to make your life more interesting.'

Simon looked up at Lorna and smiled confidently. 'Sister Parry made my leg better when I fell and hurt it. But it wasn't hurt as much as you were hurt, Daddy.'

'I'm not really hurt, Simon,' Kane said quietly. 'I should be coming home to-morrow morning. I'll find out what the doctor has to say about it.'

'And then you'll go away again and I shan't see you.' Simon's expression showed his feelings and Lorna felt a pang of sympathy for him.

'That's where you're wrong,' Kane said firmly. 'I'm not going away for a long time. You'll see the difference when I do come home. For a start I'll buy you that pony I've been promising you for months.'

Lorna saw the boy's face expand with happiness, and she felt her own emotions rise at the sight of so much candid joy.

'I don't think you really need me here while you're talking to Simon,' she said softly. 'You're doing very well on your own.'

Kane looked at her, a smile on his face, and he nodded. 'It does seem easier than it appeared to be,' he admitted. 'Thank you, Sister.'

'It's all part of the job,' Lorna told him

lightly, and departed with elation filling her. It pleased her to see the boy happy, and she knew it was because her own son was no longer living. But she was past the stage of wondering why it had to be. Both her son and her husband were gone for ever and nothing could bring them back. Admitting that fact to herself was half the battle of recovering from the tragic blow, and that was something else she knew. She returned to her work feeling more light-hearted than she had been in three years.

THREE

Returning to her office, Lorna found one of the nurses waiting for her. They sorted out some of the problems that had arisen, but Lorna discovered that she needed to concentrate in order to keep her mind upon what she was doing. Her thoughts kept slipping to Julian and Simon Kane, and she kept hoping that the two of them would find a great deal more happiness than they had shared in the past.

Then Kane's secretary returned, and Lorna glanced at her watch.

'I'll go and fetch him,' she said, smiling. 'He should be a happy boy now.'

'He was worried about his father. I only wish we'd had time this morning to settle his fears.' The secretary looked concerned. 'Simon is such a marvellous boy. He's very intelligent and forward for his age. Losing his mother set him back considerably, and I'm hoping that his father can find more time for him. The lad needs a father's touch.'

'I agree with you.' Lorna nodded. 'Perhaps life will change for Simon as a result of this accident. That sort of thing does tend to pull one up with a jolt. But perhaps the good intentions will be only short-lived. That would be a disaster for the boy.'

'I agree. But I'll see what I can do now there are cracks in the wall, so to speak. I'll wait here while you go and fetch Simon. If I see his father again he'll want to start talking business, and he should take this opportunity to snatch a complete rest.'

'I'll see that he does while he's here, but he may be discharged in the morning. However I'll fetch Simon. It must be getting near to his bed-time.'

She went along to Kane's room and found him sitting in a chair by the window with the boy on his lap. Simon was asleep, his head leaning against his father's shoulder, and she smiled gently as she went forward. Kane was gazing out at the shadowed garden. The sun had gone and the evening was closing in. The sky was cloudless, the colour of slate, and the first stars were glimmering overhead.

'Is it time already?' Kane demanded.

'I'm afraid it is.' She spoke softly, but the boy stirred and opened his eyes.

'Be a good boy until I come home, Simon,' Kane said. 'Just remember all that I've told you. I expect to see you tomorrow.'

'Goodnight, Daddy, and God bless you!' Simon arose and stretched sleepily, then came and took hold of Lorna's hand. She could see that he was barely awake, and held his chubby hand tightly as they departed.

'Sister,' Kane called as they reached the door. 'Would you spare me a few moments before you go off duty? I'd like to talk to you.'

'All right. There should be a slack period just before ten.'

They walked the length of the ward and Simon looked around wonderingly, but when they reached the office and he saw Isobel Garvin he ran to her with a little cry of delight.

'I saw Daddy and he's not going to die. He may be coming home tomorrow, Miss Isobel.'

'That's good news.' The secretary smiled as she met Lorna's gaze.

'Goodbye, Sister.' Simon turned towards Lorna. 'I hope I'll see you again. Daddy says you've been very good to us.'

'Goodbye, Simon, and I hope your Daddy will be home with you tomorrow,' Lorna replied.

She stood listening to the sound of the receding footsteps on the stairs, and the echoing sounds seemed to strike through her heart. In her mind she could hear the voice of her own son as it had sounded in the last year of his life. He had been four then, and now he would have been six. She blinked and fought against the wave of emotion which surged upwards in her mind, compressing her lips and smiling wryly as she held on. Then she turned away to busy herself with work, which seemed to be the only sedative for what ailed her. She was in the last period of her shift, and usually the last two hours passed fairly quickly. If she were not careful she would find herself with a mass of paperwork to do before she could get away.

After writing up her reports she made a final round of the patients, and paused at the door of Kane's room. Then she turned the handle and entered quietly in case he was asleep, peering at him in the darkened room.

'I'm awake, Sister,' he said, and she switched on the dim light and crossed to his bed, smoothing the covers and touching the pillows until she saw his smile. 'Still at it,' he commented. 'I wouldn't be surprised if you did that to your own bed when you get home.'

'I probably do without noticing it,' she

responded. 'I'm getting ready to go off duty now, Mr Kane, and you said something about wanting to speak to me. What can I do for you?'

'I really don't know what to say now. It's this new awareness of my son. I expect you can tell that I have rather neglected him in the past, but now I want to make it up to him and see that he lives a more normal life. He's had no real home life so far! I wanted to ask your advice. That may sound stupid of me, considering the fact that Simon has a governess and a housekeeper to help, plus my secretary. But I'm not entirely happy with the way he's being reared.'

'I don't know what to say. Surely there are female relatives who could guide you. Has Simon no aunts at all?'

'No one. Now his mother is dead I'm the only person in the world related to him. That's why I'm feeling so badly now. I dread to think what might have become of him if I had been killed last night.'

'I see what you mean.' Lorna could feel

herself being drawn into the situation as if invisible strings were attached to her mind. 'I'll do anything I can to help,' she went on, 'but I am rather at a loss for action.'

'Perhaps I'm expecting too much,' he said softly. 'You and I are strangers, but your father is my family doctor so perhaps I can draw upon that fact as a reason for talking like this. I'll do anything, regardless of cost, to give my son the best of everything. But Simon did nothing but talk of you while he was in here. I don't know why, but you certainly made a big impact upon him. I think he's missing his mother badly and no one around him has recognised the fact. You treated him very sympathetically and that is why he has inclined towards you.'

Lorna said nothing, sensing that he was leading up to a point.

'You get some free time every day, don't you?' he enquired. 'Would I be presuming too much to ask you to visit Cairn Manor one morning? I confess quite brazenly that I've been asking some questions about you today and learned a lot. I know you are not romantically entangled with anyone, not even Foster, although he's been trying hard to interest you. May I take up a little of your time, Sister?'

'I don't quite know what to say.' Lorna gazed into his dark eyes and realized that he was deadly serious.

'It's certainly not for my sake,' he added with some of the old sharpness coming into his tone. 'But I feel you might have a great influence on Simon and he needs guidance.'

'If you put it like that then I don't see how I could refuse,' said Lorna, and it seemed to her that a stranger was speaking from her mind.

'Good.' He smiled, his pale face brightening. 'I'll call you in a couple of days. You're on this particular shift for the rest of this week, aren't you?'

'That's right. I go off duty at ten on Friday evening and I'm free until six on Monday morning.'

'Then may I call you before the week-end

to ask if you can spend Saturday or Sunday at the Manor?' Interest thickened his voice.

Lorna drew a swift breath as she considered her reply, for she had the feeling that this was one of the fateful moments of her life. 'All right,' she said softly. 'I'll expect you to telephone.'

'Thank you.' He was smiling now. 'Simon will be pleased.'

Lorna departed, feeling as if she were caught up in the throes of a strange dream. For the past three years she had lived in a rut that had been running over with grief and loneliness, but suddenly her thoughts of the past seemed less sharper than usual, and she was amazed, as she prepared to go off duty, to find that some of the dark clouds that had seemed to hang over her life ever since the tragic event were beginning to fade.

Had she reached the natural moment when her feelings would begin to rise once more, when grief had at last decided to relent? She had often been told that time would heal her pain. She had never believed that it could happen in her case, but now she was not so sure, and as she left the hospital she began to hope that the grim past was really behind her and finally out of the clutches of her grasping mind.

But a figure stepped in front of her as she walked along the path towards the main gate, and she firmed her lips as she took in Jack Foster's powerful figure.

'I thought I'd wait for you,' he said before she could speak. 'You must be tired after that long shift, especially with a man like Julian Kane for a patient. Did you have any more trouble with him, by the way?'

'I didn't. I fancy that perhaps I put him into his place.' She smiled as she spoke, but said no more.

'I know his type. His kind always make the worst patients. But he'll be discharged tomorrow morning, thank Heaven! We can do without his kind around.'

'And I can do without you stopping me getting home after a long, hard shift,' she countered, trying to step around him, but he moved with her, preventing her escape.

'You're not getting away as easily as that,' he remonstrated.

'Anything wrong, Lorna?' demanded a voice at her back, and she looked around to find her mother standing there. 'Oh, it's you, Jack,' continued Mrs Parry. 'I thought Lorna was being accosted. I came to pick you up, dear, thinking that you would appreciate a lift.'

'That was all I was offering her,' retorted Foster, scowling. 'Very well.' He turned away. 'Better luck next time. Goodnight.'

'He doesn't seem to be in a very good mood,' observed Mrs Parry.

'That's because you've stopped him in the middle of one of his attempts to persuade me to go out with him.' Lorna chuckled. 'But he'll get over it. Where's the car? I'll be relieved to get home tonight. It's been a hard day.'

'This way.' Mrs Parry led the way out to the street, chatting all the time, but Lorna did not attempt to make conversation, and sat slumped in the car while her mother drove homeward. After a glance at her, Mrs Parry fell silent.

Home was a large, detached house on the outskirts of town. There were lights on in the lounge, and Lorna drooped with tiredness as she alighted from the car. They entered the house and she kicked off her shoes, then put on her slippers, sighing in relief as she did so. Her legs ached and her whole body seemed drained of vitality. Mrs Parry led the way into the lounge, and Lorna saw that her father was not at home. She sat down, her slim shoulders sagging with weariness.

'Father went out around eight and hasn't come back yet. I think old Mr Cummings is dying. He was very ill with pneumonia yesterday but he wouldn't be sent into hospital. Do you want something to eat?'

'No thank you. I'm going to take a shower and go to bed.'

'You must have something to eat.' Mrs

Parry was medium-sized, getting plump now, at fifty-five. Her blue eyes were extremely pale, and glistened like glass as she regarded Lorna. 'You do look tired – more so than usual. I'll go and run the bath for you.'

'No, don't bother. I'll just take a shower instead. What can you tell me about Julian Kane, Mother?'

'Julian Kane!' Mrs Parry sat down on the settee and gazed at Lorna. 'The one who lives at Cairn Manor?'

'Yes. He was in a road accident last night and was in my ward today.' Lorna's blue eyes shadowed as she recalled the events of the day.

'He's one of your father's patients. From all accounts he's a very odd man. Very rich, but his wife died in mysterious circumstances, as they say.'

'Did Father attend her when she died?'

'He was called in, as he always is when someone dies unnaturally. I recall him talking about it. I think it must have been three years ago at least.'

'I was away at the time, on a course in London,' said Lorna.

'That's right. But was he seriously injured?'

'No. He'll probably be discharged tomorrow. He had some slight injuries to his head. I met his son today. Poor child! He's about six years old.'

'That's a significant age, isn't it?' Mrs Parry frowned as she gazed into Lorna's eyes. 'Don't become involved with Julian Kane because of his son, Lorna. I was a Nursing Sister, remember, and I learned that the first golden rule is never to become involved with your patients.'

'I've always stuck to that rule,' Lorna said quietly. 'But Simon Kane isn't one of my patients, and his father won't be after tomorrow. I've agreed to go out to Cairn Manor to see Simon at the week-end.'

'Really!' Mrs Parry was surprised. 'Well this is the best news I've heard in a long time.'

'But you just said I shouldn't become involved with Julian Kane,' protested Lorna.

'That was different. If you're going to meet him socially then all well and good. Your father and I have been worried about you, Lorna. It's time you recovered from your tragedy.'

Lorna felt her face stiffen a little, but, surprisingly, the cold pang that usually struck through her breast at the mention of her loss was not apparent now, and she wondered about it.

'I think I've got over it,' she announced.

'Then find your old friends. Julian Kane is better than nothing, but for preference you can't beat your old friends. Why don't you bring Jack Foster home this week-end? He's been showing great interest in you ever since he came to Rossglen.'

'Now wait a moment, Mother,' Lorna said hastily. 'I've got no interest in any man, least of all Julian Kane. I'm only going to try and help his son. I felt so sorry for him.'

'Don't fool yourself, Lorna.' Mrs Parry

spoke in stern tones. 'It may start off with your interest in the boy, but if you see much of Kane himself then you'll become interested in him. I've seen him, and he's handsome enough to turn any girl's head.'

'I'm not any girl, Mother.'

'Apart from that, he's highly successful in business, and Cairn Manor has been in his family for generations. They say he must be a millionaire! But his character is suspect, Lorna, and that's what concerns me most. His wife died on the moors, and it was said that he knew more about it than ever came out at the inquest.'

Lorna smiled. 'You're getting quite worried, Mother,' she said. 'All I'm planning to do is spend a day at Cairn Manor.'

'I wouldn't dissuade you seeing him, Lorna, especially after what you've been through. I do hope this is the turning point for you.'

Lorna suppressed a sigh. 'Look, I'm going to take a shower and go to bed,' she said firmly. 'I can hardly keep my eyes open and

I feel as if I've been on duty nonstop for a week. I must be getting old!'

She left the room before her mother could continue the conversation and ascended the stairs to her bedroom, tiredly removing her uniform and preparing to take a shower. Her mind was filled with a sense of strangeness that she could not comprehend, and by the time she got into bed she still had not come to terms with her thoughts.

FOUR

Next morning Lorna awoke early and lay thinking idly about the events of the previous day. Sunlight bathed the room and she raised herself to peer out through the open window. The sky was clear and very blue, the breeze warm. The middle of May was perfect and she felt a wistful longing for a holiday, when she could relax and forget the grim business of nursing.

She dragged herself from her thoughts and thrust her feelings into the background. Showering and dressing leisurely with the knowledge that she would be going on duty in the afternoon, but with no intention of doing anything strenuous before duty, she went down to breakfast and found her parents at the table.

William Parry was tall and spare, with

dark eyes that regarded Lorna very care-
fully. At fifty-eight he was well set in his
professional life, but seemed at least ten
years younger than his true age. Lorna went
to his side and kissed his cheek as she
greeted him. His brown eyes glinted as he
glanced up at her.

'Hello, Lorna,' he greeted cheerfully.
'You're looking spry this morning.'

'Spry?' She kissed her mother and sat
down at the table. Mrs Mulloch, the
housekeeper, peered into the room and
called out a cheerful hello.

'I'll have your breakfast ready for you in a
few moments, Miss Lorna,' she called
blithely.

'I was telling your father about Julian
Kane,' said Mrs Parry, pouring Lorna a cup
of tea.

'That reminds me, Father.' Lorna didn't
want to start a discussion on her arrangements with Julian Kane. 'Mr Kane would
like you to call on him today when you're in
his area. He's worried about his son.'

'I thought you said you saw the boy at the hospital yesterday?' asked Mrs Parry.

'He's not physically ill. I gather the father is concerned about the boy's mental health.' Lorna's cheeks burned a little as her father's penetrating gaze lifted to her face. 'Not that he's afraid the boy is going insane, or anything like it. But the child has been alone for some time and he's concerned about his welfare.'

'I'll be in that area this afternoon. I'll call at the Manor.' William Parry set down his cup and glanced at his watch. He sighed heavily. 'It's almost time I left,' he commented. 'How's work at the hospital, Lorna?'

'Fine, just fine. The only thing is, I'm beginning to feel exhausted at the end of a shift.' She smiled. 'I must be getting old.'

'Wait until you're my age and then see how you feel at the end of a long day,' he retorted.

'I don't know how you manage,' said Lorna, smiling, relieved that the subject had been changed.

Mrs Mulloch brought in her breakfast and she began to eat. Within a few moments her father got to his feet, excused himself, and departed to start his day. Mrs Parry remained opposite Lorna, watching her closely.

'You have changed a great deal,' the older woman suddenly remarked. 'I hadn't noticed it before, but you're emerging from the darkness and walking in the sunshine again. It's taken you a long time to get over it, Lorna.'

'I feel as if it is in the past now,' Lorna replied, and waited for the habitual pang to strike through her. But this time it did not occur, and she blinked as she considered the fact.

'I hope things will work out for you.' Mrs Parry paused, her face showing anxiety. 'I'm concerned about you.'

'Well you needn't be. I can take care of myself. I'm twenty-eight years old, not a teenager who can have her head turned by an attractive male and lots of money.'

'I wasn't thinking quite along those lines.'

'It's all right, Mother.' Lorna smiled. 'I'm teasing you. I know how you feel about me. The Lord knows you have reason to worry about me. My life was completely shattered three years ago and I'm only now beginning to recover from it. But I'll be all right. Life is like that! People have a way of getting on top again. At least I have my health, and that's the most important thing. That much I have learned from my work.'

'What are you going to do this morning?' Now Mrs Parry seemed keen to change the subject. 'I was planning on going shopping. Would you care to go with me?'

'Not this morning.' Lorna shook her head. 'I feel lazy today. I'm on duty at two, and between now and then I'm just going to take things easy. It looks like a nice day so I think I'll get out a deck chair and do some sun-worshipping.'

'Are you sure you're not sickening for something?' For a moment concern showed in Mrs Parry's face. 'I've never known you to willingly sit still for more than five minutes at a time.'

'I told you, I'm getting old.' Lorna was already thinking of Julian Kane and Simon. 'But if you're not using the car I might take myself off for a drive.'

'To look over Cairn Manor?' demanded Mrs Parry.

Lorna gazed at her mother, then sighed and smiled. 'I could never fool you, could I? Very well. I must admit that was in my mind. But it's not Julian Kane I'm interested in, it's his son. I felt so sorry for him yesterday.'

'But what can you do, dear? You have your job at the hospital. You couldn't spend much time with the child, and if you did make friends with him it couldn't possibly last. He would miss you sorely the moment you stopped seeing him.'

'I hadn't thought of that,' admitted Lorna. 'Nothing is ever simple, is it? But I can't even explain why I should get so interested.

It just evolved.'

'You're beginning to think that fate is taking a hand in your life, is that it?' Mrs Parry nodded wisely. 'Well I wouldn't sneer at that suggestion. I think you deserve a helping hand from whatever controls our destinies. You've had your share of suffering and deserve a great deal of happiness. My heart has bled for you.'

'It has been a nightmare,' admitted Lorna. 'Putting on a front that didn't show emotion when all the time I felt like sobbing; nursing people who seemed to be burdened with as much tragedy as myself! But I do feel as if I'm coming out of it now, and I want to try and relax and forget the horror of it.'

'I understand, but you could land yourself in worse trouble.'

'I don't see how anything could be worse than losing a family.'

'You could fall in love with the wrong type of man.'

Lorna smiled and shook her head. 'I don't think I could ever fall in love again,' she declared. 'I have a very absorbing job and I'm comfortable in the rut that I've made for myself.'

'Well if you do make any mistakes then I hope they won't be major ones.' Mrs Parry smiled.

'Then may I use the car this morning?' asked Lorna, her eyes glistening.

'Certainly. Go and enjoy yourself.'

Lorna dressed casually for the excursion, wearing a short, pink skirt and a white lace blouse. She went out to the garage. Her father's Rover was gone but the white Triumph Herald she and her mother used was parked inside, and there was a sense of great anticipation in her mind as she drove away from the house.

The morning was peaceful and warm and she was encompassed by an oddly satisfying sense of wellbeing as she drove out of the suburbs of Rossglen and headed along the lonely road that led eventually to the Highland village of Braeside. But Cairn Manor was situated in a glen between two mountains, and the road, although well-surfaced was narrow and twisting. Lorna stared ahead, afraid of meeting a car coming from the opposite direction.

There were patches of mist, ghostly and ethereal in the sunlight, and the growing heat of the morning was trying to catch them. They changed their shapes intangibly as if spiritual fingers were manipulating them, and the faint breeze sent them rising quickly into oblivion.

But she hardly saw the wild mountain country about her, the bare slopes of the Highlands. Gigantic rocks and crumbling hill-sides reared up on all sides, lonely, desolate, inhabited only by sheep and cattle. She was thinking of Julian and Simon Kane, and already her mind seemed to be in a whirl of unstable conjecture.

She had driven out this way many times during her off-duty hours, and the wild, majestic beauty of the scenery never failed to touch a nerve of appreciation inside her. The road turned sharply to the right and dived steeply into a ravine. It skirted a madly rushing stream that gurgled and hurled itself over dark, jagged rocks and tumbled helter-skelter around larger slabs of stone – sometimes cascading through bright space, glittering in the sunlight.

The ravine widened unexpectedly into Glen Cairn, and there in the distance, situated upon a remote prominence, was Cairn Manor. Lorna stopped the car at the side of the road overlooking a quiet salmon pool that had the glittering surface of a mirror, and the surrounding rowan trees were pictured intricately upon the reflecting face of the water. She breathed deeply of the bright, sweet air and felt a rush of emotion that threatened to overwhelm her senses. She seemed scarcely able to contain the impressions that rushed upon her with as much force as the stream gurgling in the background, and breathed deeply and clenched her hands, feeling as if life had suddenly opened up for her but was threatening to close in once more after giving her a slight glimpse of Heaven.

She compressed her lips as she fought the fear of losing her grip upon that blessed sense of relief, and sensed that she was standing upon the threshold of great change. She wanted that more than anything. Three years of living under a cloud, in the grey shadows of grief, had taken great toll of her happiness and optimism, but this sunny morning was rejuvenating her jaded senses. She began to look forward into the future with hope rather than retain the bad habit of looking backwards into the past.

The Manor attracted her attention and she gazed at its four-square outline. From the distance she could not make out much of its detail, but the roof was turreted like a miniature castle, and it seemed solid upon its hard rock base.

Above the house and in the background, the wall of the glen heightened roughly, permitting only brief glimpses of the more majestic mountains beyond. A sense of remoteness struck through Lorna, and haunting silence descended upon her, bringing a sense of peace which she had almost forgotten existed.

She could see the road twisting towards the big house, and although she dearly wanted to go on a stiffness inserted itself into her mind. Perhaps it was pride which forbade her to continue. But she felt afraid of letting herself be seen near the house. She did not want anyone to get the idea that she was intent upon gaining admittance to the Kane family circle.

But she drove on slowly, following the road. Suddenly a bird flew into the windscreen with a sickening thud, stunning itself, and she clenched her teeth as she looked into the rear view mirror and saw it fluttering upon the ground. Stopping hurriedly, she alighted and went back, but when she reached the bird it was dead, and for a moment she stood holding the slight feathered body in her hands, her thoughts sombre.

In the midst of all this wild beauty there was death. So it was with life generally. She felt a strand of intangible mental agony drift across her mind but fought it. Death awaited everyone, and the incontrovertible fact was that it came in untimely fashion to some people.

She placed the bird gently on the verge, determined not to let her morbid attitude reassert itself. Time had healed the scars considerably, although she knew they would never completely disappear. Life had to go on, and she impressed that fact upon herself as she returned to the car.

As she drew nearer Cairn Manor she subjected it to a closer study. She had driven past it many times before, but never had it seemed to hold so much special interest. A mountain stream that was in a hurry to join the burn in the valley was muttering its tortuous way through the grey rocks with insistent musical sound, and a perfectly arched little bridge carried the narrow road across it. Then the road widened and a turn-off ended abruptly at a pair of closed black iron gates. She halted the car and gazed through the railings at the lofty stone house.

Sunlight glinted on some of the many windows in the wide face of the building, and they seemed like dead eyes staring at her. Lorna suppressed a shiver, thinking of Simon Kane living in such a mausoleum of a home, then smiled gently as she pictured the boy's appealing face. Birds were singing in the surrounding trees and a faint breeze rustled through the foliage.

Lorna could not prevent a wondering sigh from coursing through her, and dragged herself from deep thoughts and glanced at her watch. Reality was for ever in the background, nudging imperceptibly with timely reminders of duty, and she realized that time was indeed flitting swiftly by.

Somewhere in the distance a dog barked and echoes flew, causing birds to flutter out of the trees. Lorna fancied she heard a child's voice shouting, but although she stared intently at the grounds surrounding the mansion she failed to detect movement anywhere.

She drove on, following the road slowly, glancing back repeatedly, feeling a strange reluctance to leave the spot. A low stone wall surrounded the estate and she could see over it as she continued. Then the road began to meander away from the perimeter of the estate and she stopped the car once more in a convenient spot and got out to gaze at another profile of the Kane home.

Presently she caught a glimpse of movement across the parkland that stretched from the wall to the house. A dog appeared briefly in the bushes skirting a pool. Lorna saw a bright yellow ball bouncing away on the grass, thrown by someone out of sight, and the dog, a Border Collie, pounced upon it as though it were a fox worrying sheep. A child's voice rang out echoingly in joyous laughter.

Lorna assumed that Simon was at play, and a gentle smile touched her lips as she considered their chance meeting the day before. She walked along the outside of the wall for several yards, hoping to catch a glimpse of the child, but although she could see the glint of water beyond the bushes she could not see the boy. The dog was barking furiously now, nosing the ball around, unable to pick it up in its sensitive mouth.

Then Simon appeared, running after the dog and snatching up the ball. The boy was fully absorbed in his game, and Lorna watched intently, smiling because he was enjoying himself.

The dog jumped up and around the small figure as Simon lifted the ball high out of the animal's reach, barking as if its life depended upon the noise, and Lorna shook her head slowly. She could understand Simon's loneliness, playing with a ball and a dog in such quiet solitude.

But the next instant the scene of happy recreation was changed abruptly. The barking dog leaped for the ball held out so teasingly by the enraptured child, but changed direction in mid-air as Simon switched the ball from one hand to the other. The animal collided heavily with the slight figure, knocking Simon off balance and seizing its chance to grab the ball.

Lorna was horrified to see Simon stagger backwards, tripping and falling over a concealed root to sprawl completely out of sight amongst the bushes. The next moment there was a terrified scream and a heavy splash!

The echoes of the splash faded before Lorna could break the paralysis of shock that gripped her. The dog turned and left the ball, disappearing into the bushes fringing the pool, but now its bark contained a note of frantic appeal. Lorna drew a deep breath and sprang at the wall, hurling herself over it with reckless abandon, falling heavily inside the grounds and hurting her knees and an elbow. She pushed herself upright and ran towards the pool, her mind a hideous playground for ominous fears.

When she burst through the bushes she almost went headlong into the water. She halted, breathless and shaken, and frowned as she looked around for Simon. The dog was standing on the bank, peering into the rippled water, and it took no notice of Lorna despite the fact that she was a trespassing stranger.

Peering into the pool, stark horror speared through Lorna when she saw the indistinct shape of a child's figure down in the murky depths of the pool. She kicked off her shoes without pausing to consider and took a deep breath as she hurled herself into the water. Hitting the surface hard, she went down into the cold, greenish depths, her mind warning that this was very deep. The water was blurred by her entrance and she stuck out blindly for the spot where she had seen the pale figure. But her outstretched hands encountered nothing as she swam around strongly.

She came back to the surface for air and looked around quickly, dashing water out of her eyes. There was no sign of the boy, and the surface was still disturbed, making vision almost impossible. Panic began to flare in her mind and she clenched her teeth as a chill pang struck through her heart. Holding her breath, she dived again, aiming once more for the spot where she had seen the boy's figure.

Lorna's eyes were wide open as she swam, looking for anything that resembled a child. It was gloomy in the depths, although the bright sunlight aided her somewhat restricted vision, but her lungs were near to bursting point, and she had started back once more to the surface when she spotted a pale shape just ahead. She grasped at it with both hands, felt the thin fabric of a shirt in her fingers, and clutched desperately as she shot upwards, gasping for air when her head broke the surface.

Simon's body came up with her, limp and apparently lifeless, the small face ashen, the mouth open, lips stiff. Gasping heavily, Lorna propelled herself to the bank, where the dog was now howling in a most horrifying manner. Aware that time was vital, she hastened to get out of the water, but the bank was high, the sides wet and slippery. She grasped Simon and tried to thrust him upwards on to the bank, but she sank into the water under the effort and rapidly tired, her limbs feeling heavy and awkward.

The dog reached down and took hold of Simon's shirt in its teeth, tugging savagely. Lorna felt a spurt of hope as she thrust from below. But the unconscious child was only halfway out of the water when the shirt tore out of the dog's teeth and Simon came tumbling back into the pool on top of Lorna.

Frantic now, Lorna held the small body tightly and peered around, looking for a lower part of the bank, but it seemed that she was at the lowest point. Taking a deep breath, she tried to work out some plan that would avail her.

But in the background there were shouting voices, and she became slowly aware of the fact. She called for help, desperation in her tone, and a moment later two men came pushing through the bushes. Lorna was astounded to see that one of them was Julian Kane, pale of face and unsteady. The other was dressed in a chauffeur's uniform.

Kane almost came into the pool himself as he reached down and grasped his apparently lifeless son. Lorna gasped with relief as the boy's dead weight was taken off her arms, and the next instant the chauffeur had grasped her hands and Lorna was lifted bodily out of the water.

Lorna staggered to where Kane had laid the boy on the grass and fell to her knees beside him. He looked at her, his features unbelievably pale, his dark eyes glazed with horror.

'I saw you running across the grass as we drove in through the gates,' he said harshly. 'Is he dead?'

Lorna made no reply. She pushed him aside, sprawling in her weakness, and her breathing was ragged as she turned Simon upon his back and began to work desperately upon the child. She tried to hold her fears at bay as she used the kiss of life.

Kane's laboured breathing in Lorna's ears as she worked unceasingly brought home to her the reality of the situation, but in the background she could hear a woman's voice calling Simon's name. Kane said something to the chauffeur and the man's footsteps sounded heavy upon the firm ground as he departed hurriedly.

Lorna was beginning to feel deathly cold inside, for there was no response from the apparently lifeless boy. She could feel the coldness of Simon's mouth against her own, and prayed incessantly as she worked, maintaining exact timing, putting every-thing she knew into the desperate effort.

'Oh, God, don't let him die!' Julian Kane's voice was harsh and imploring at Lorna's side, and emotion flooded her as she persisted in her efforts to put life back into the child's cold body. Time seemed to freeze, and Lorna sensed the dreadful presence of death at her shoulder, just watching and waiting to snatch away this precious young life that was in the balance. She thought of her own lost son as she worked, and determination filled her. Death would not win this time!

Then there was a tremor in the small body, and Lorna felt a muscular contraction in the neat mouth pressed against her own. She continued to work until she became aware that Simon was breathing again. Easing back from the boy, she sagged limply at his side, and heard the boy's moaning breath rising and falling irregularly as blackness filled her eyes and thankfulness swept through her.

Lorna looked up at Kane and saw the naked agony in his face. There was horror indelibly painted on his handsome features and his eyes were filled with tears.

'He's breathing!' Lorna whispered. 'He'll be all right. Wrap him in your coat and get him into the house as quickly as you can.'

'Thank God!' Kane said fervently, and leaned forward and kissed Lorna's wet mouth.

FIVE

Lorna was overwhelmed with emotion as the chauffeur returned, followed by a worried-looking Isobel Garvin. Simon was wrapped in a coat and the chauffeur carried him away. Kane took hold of Lorna's arm and they hurried to the drive where the car waited. Simon was placed on Lorna's lap when she was seated in the car and Kane entered at her side. They drove quickly to the house, and as Lorna looked down into the boy's ashen face some of her shock began to lift and she felt as if she were awakening from a nightmare.

A shocked silence surrounded them as they took Simon into the house. Lorna could feel her knees trembling. She was barefoot and trembling, shivering more from shock than from the cold water, and when Simon was placed on a couch and covered with a blanket she examined the boy and satisfied herself that he would be all right.

Kane stood watching her silently, his face grey and taut, his eyes wide and intense. The chauffeur and Isobel Garvin stood near, and the housekeeper appeared, demanding to be told what had happened.

'Leave us alone,' Kane suddenly muttered. 'Get some hot water bottles, Mrs Heywood.'

'Shall I call the doctor?' demanded Isobel, her eyes on Lorna's haggard face.

'Sister Parry is expert enough for me,' Kane said. 'She's already saved Simon's life. I'll talk to you later, Isobel. I shall want to know why Simon was alone at the pool after all the warnings that were given.'

The secretary departed instantly, followed by the chauffeur, and the housekeeper hurried away, closing the door at her back. Lorna stood by Simon's side, feeling for his pulse, and she raised her eyes until she met

Kane's hard gaze.

'He almost died!' said Kane. His lips looked blue with shock. 'By God, now I know what you must have experienced in your tragedy! Is he going to be all right now?'

'He's badly shocked, but I think he'll be all right. We could take him to the hospital for a check-up, if you wish. They would probably keep him in for observation. That water he swallowed might be bad.'

'I'll ring for an ambulance,' he said, and turned away. He left the room, walking with unsteady strides, and Lorna watched him, her own mind attempting to regain the initiative from shock.

She looked down at the child, now breathing heavily, and relived the dreadful moments of rescue. Shaking her head slowly, she fought down the fears that invaded her mind. If Simon had drowned! If she had not decided to drive out this way today! If she hadn't met Simon yesterday at the hospital! The frightening possibilities teemed through her brain and she felt strangely weak. She sat down on the couch beside the boy and lowered her head into her hands. Her mouth tingled, but not so much from having administered the kiss of life as from the brief contact Julian Kane had made with her.

The first she knew of Kane's return was his hand upon her shoulder.

'I'm sorry,' he said as she looked up at him. 'In my shock I'd forgotten about your welfare. I don't for the life of me know how you were there at the time, but I'm never going to question fate again. You saved my son's life and I'll be for ever in your debt. What were you doing out here?'

'I was driving by,' she replied slowly, trying to sound casual. 'I'm off duty until two, as you know. I spotted Simon from the road, playing with a ball and the dog.' She explained what had occurred.

'If I live to be a hundred and see you every day until I die I'll never be able to thank you enough,' he retorted. He took her by the shoulders and gazed intently into her eyes. 'I had a very strange feeling yesterday when I met you. I can't explain it even now. But something seemed to happen to my mind, and it was as if I sensed you'd become important. It was uncanny, and perhaps I'm making a fool of myself for saying it, but after what happened this morning I have to tell you about it.'

Lorna was silent, recalling her own sharp feelings at the moment of meeting Simon, and she wondered if her uneasiness earlier that morning had been a presentiment. Had something beyond her usual awareness prompted her to drive out to look at Cairn Manor? But she was too emotionally upset to be able to think clearly, and steeled herself against the reaction which threatened to strike through her.

'It's high time we thought about you,' he said, turning as the housekeeper entered the room carrying two hot water bottles. 'Mrs Heywood, run a hot bath for Sister Parry, then see if you can find her something suitable to change into.' He looked at Lorna again. 'I'll drive you home after Simon has been taken to hospital. I'll get you a brandy. You look badly shaken, and I know I could do with a drink after what I've witnessed. I don't know how I'm ever going to be able to thank you for what you've done.'

'I don't need any thanks,' Lorna said shakily. 'I'm thanking God right now for allowing me to be in the right place at the right time.'

She took the bottles from the housekeeper, a small, bird-like woman whose piercing brown eyes seemed to cut right through her, and placed them under the blanket beside the child. Simon stirred as he was touched, then opened his eyes and looked up at Lorna. Kane came to Lorna's side, gazing down at his son over her shoulder.

'How are you feeling, Simon?' he demanded.

'I fell into the water, Daddy.'

'Sister Parry saw you fall in and she

pulled you out.'

'I jumped in after you,' Lorna said lightly. 'At least it was a nice day for swimming.'

'You were told never to go near that pool, young man,' Kane said in severe tones.

'I had nothing else to do, Daddy. I wanted to come to the hospital to meet you but they wouldn't let me. And I wanted to see Sister Parry again.'

'Well you've seen her again, and under circumstances I hope will never be repeated. Sister Parry will be coming to see you again, Simon, probably at the end of the week. But right now she must take a hot bath and get out of her wet clothes. An ambulance is coming to take you to hospital for a check-up.'

'Shall I see you there, Sister Parry?' the boy demanded.

'Yes, if you're still there when I go on duty,' Lorna said with a smile. She was shaken, her nerves unsteady, but she was recovering from the shock of the incident and hoped that Simon was also coming out

103

of it all right.

'We've got to try and think of a satisfactory way to say "thank you" to Sister Parry for saving your life, Simon,' Kane said.

'The water got in my mouth,' the boy commented. 'It was nasty.'

'Don't worry about it now.' Lorna stroked his damp forehead, then arose. 'I'll see you later, Simon. You lie there and rest now, and soon you'll be as well as you were before it happened. But promise me you'll never play near the pool again.'

'I promise. I was lucky you were there, wasn't I?'

'You don't know just how lucky,' Kane said fervently.

Lorna smiled as she followed the housekeeper out of the room and up to a bathroom. Her legs were still trembling, she discovered, but fancied that a hot bath would soon restore her. Mrs Heywood glanced at her, and there was a brightness in the older woman's dark gaze.

'I know you well, Sister Parry,' she said in a high-pitched tone. 'You're the doctor's daughter, and it was a miracle that you happened to be passing in your car when the boy fell into the water.'

'I wasn't actually passing,' Lorna said, feeling awkward. 'I had stopped to look at the house. It's one of my favourite scenes. I saw Simon playing, and was watching him when he fell into the pool.'

'And you're a strong swimmer, no doubt! It was Providence arranged it. That poor bairn has no mother and there's no one in the whole wide world who cares a fig what might happen to him. I'm thinking that you haven't heard the last of this little episode.'

'I don't need thanks for what I did,' Lorna said as she was shown into a bathroom. 'My whole life consists of taking care of people – trying to save life. I'm thankful that I was on hand today.'

'I'll try to find you other clothes while your own are drying. In the meantime there's a dressing gown on the inside of the door you can use. There's plenty of hot water, and you'd better be quick getting into it for I can fair hear your teeth chattering now.'

'That's shock, not cold,' Lorna explained.

'I'll lay out some clothes for you in that bedroom opposite, if you'll go over there when you've bathed. I'll see that your car is brought to the house, Sister.'

'Thank you, Mrs Heywood.'

The old housekeeper departed and Lorna took a bath then wrapped herself in the dressing gown and went across to the bedroom Mrs Heywood had indicated. She found a black skirt, a pink blouse, and some underwear laid out on a bed, and dressed quickly in them, wondering who owned them. There was a tap at the door and Isobel Garvin entered.

'I see that my clothes fit you fairly well,' the secretary observed.

'Are they yours? Thank you for letting me borrow them.'

'It's the least I could do after what you did. If anything had happened to Simon Mr

Kane would have had my life.' For a moment there was silence and they regarded each other. 'What exactly were you doing outside the estate, Sister?'

'Enjoying my off-duty hours.' Lorna smiled, trying not to let her intuition have its way. A tiny voice was trying to tell her that Isobel was interested in Julian Kane and was suspicious of her own intentions. 'It happens that I often drive up this way to look at the scenery. Although I'm not a true Scot – my mother is Scottish but my father is Welsh – I do have something of my mother's blood in me that makes me want to live in these Highland surroundings. I can never see enough of this scenery.'

'Mrs Kane was like that,' Isobel said softly. 'She loved the scenery and went off on her own a great deal. I didn't know her personally. I became Mr Kane's secretary after she died on the moors. But I've heard Perkins, the chauffeur, talk about her.'

'It was tragic, the way she died,' Lorna agreed softly.

107

'If you're ready now I'll take you down to the morning room. Simon has gone off to hospital with his father in attendance, and I've been instructed to see you home then go on to the hospital to pick him up.'

'I have my car somewhere, thank you. I can drive myself home. I don't want to be a trouble to anyone.'

'My dear girl! After what you've done this morning you can have Cairn Manor if you want it!' There was a sudden glitter in the secretary's eyes as she studied Lorna.

'That's the last thing I should want,' Lorna replied smoothly.

'Aren't you interested in Julian Kane? I gained the impression yesterday that you might be. But if you're thinking of getting to him through his son then you'll have your work cut out. Of course, what happened this morning weighs heavily in your favour. He's beginning to realize that Simon is all he has in the world.'

'I'm afraid you're greatly mistaken,' Lorna said stiffly, and saw the girl smile thinly. 'Mr

Kane is a stranger to me. I had never seen him before yesterday.'

'He's an attractive man, and extremely wealthy. That's enough to turn any girl's head. You're not the type to go around with men, so I've learned. But with Julian Kane one can be prepared to make an exception.'

'Is that how you feel about him?' asked Lorna, her face burning. 'I assure you that I have no interest in him. Did you bring my shoes from the pool? If my car is outside then I'll leave.'

'Don't be upset, Sister. I'm accustomed to seeing women trying to hook my employer. There's been a number of them since Mrs Kane died.' Isobel smiled. 'I expect I shall be seeing you around here again despite your reaction. Your shoes are down in the hall and your car is outside the front door.'

'Thank you. I'll return your clothes as soon as possible.' Lorna started for the stairs, her face wearing a frown.

'It doesn't matter. They're old clothes. I was going to throw them out.'

Lorna descended the staircase and found her shoes. Mrs Heywood appeared as she slipped them on.

'I'm drying your wet clothes, Sister,' she said. 'Shall I send them on to you later?'

'I'll take them with me.' Lorna made an effort to keep her emotions under control. She was aware that Isobel Garvin was watching her from the top of the stairs. The secretary was obviously jealous of her, and it made her wonder exactly what kind of a relationship the girl had with Julian Kane. But it was none of her business, she told herself as she waited for the housekeeper to put her wet clothes into a plastic bag.

'I'm sure Mr Kane will be in touch with you as soon as he can get around to it,' Mrs Heywood said. 'He looked like death itself when you brought the poor wee bairn into the house.'

'We were all badly shocked,' Lorna agreed. 'Goodbye now, Mrs Heywood. I must hurry or I shall be late getting on duty.'

The housekeeper saw her to the door, and

Lorna sighed heavily as she went out to her car. Horror still gripped her. She felt weak and cold inside, and for a few moments found it difficult to concentrate upon her driving. But once she was on the open road she hastened back to town.

Mrs Parry was on the terrace when Lorna drew up in front of the house, and Lorna compressed her lips as she alighted from the car. Carrying the plastic bag containing her own clothes, she tried to hurry into the house without attracting her mother's attention.

'You've changed your clothes since leaving the house this morning,' said Mrs Parry, frowning.

Lorna reluctantly explained what had happened, and saw a mixture of horror, concern and relief flit across her mother's face. But she excused herself on the grounds of being late and hurried to her room to prepare for duty. Mrs Parry followed, asking a number of questions until Lorna had changed into her uniform and they went down to lunch.

The telephone rang while Lorna was eating the meal and Mrs Parry went in answer, to return a moment later.

'It's Julian Kane for you, Lorna.'

Lorna felt her heart give a strange little jump as she arose and went into the hall, and her pulses seemed to race as she lifted the receiver and gave her name.

'Sister, this is Julian Kane. They're keeping Simon in hospital until this evening at the earliest. But he's all right, thanks to you. I didn't get the opportunity to thank you properly before you left the Manor. I'd like to see you and talk to you.'

'I'm going on duty very shortly and I'll be on duty until ten,' she replied. 'But you don't have to thank me, Mr Kane. I'm very grateful that I was there when I was needed.'

'I'll be going into the hospital this afternoon to see Simon. May I come along to your ward to talk to you?'

'Certainly.' She felt a wave of emotion thrill through her, and her hands trembled.

Then she recalled the secretary's words and controlled herself. A frown touched her smooth forehead as she wondered why she was getting so emotional.

'I'll look in on you this afternoon then,' he said. 'I'm still trying to figure out how I can thank you for what you did. Simon is all I have in the world, and he means everything to me. I didn't realize that until I had this accident.' He paused. 'But you must be pushed for time so I'll let you go. I'll see you later.'

'Goodbye,' she responded, and went thoughtfully back into the dining room.

When she was ready to leave for the hospital her nerves were almost back to normal and some of the grim horror of the incident had faded from her mind. As she went out to the terrace a car drew up in front of the house, and Lorna stared at a stranger whose face seemed vaguely familiar. He came towards her, smiling expectantly.

'Good afternoon, Sister Parry,' he greeted.

'I'm Kenneth Sprague of the *Rossglen News*. I've heard that you saved Julian Kane's son from drowning this morning. Would you care to fill me in on some of the details?'

'Oh!' Lorna gazed at him in some surprise. 'How on earth did you get hold of that?'

He smiled and shrugged. 'We have our ways and means. I want to write up the story. You're not averse to a little publicity, are you? It's all good copy for the newspaper, and your friends and the people in this area should learn of the heroine in their midst.'

'I'm certainly no heroine! I can swim very well and I do have certificates for life-saving, so there was nothing to it. If I were a poor swimmer or couldn't swim at all and saved the child then it would be something to write about.'

'You're too modest. I'm going to splash this all over the front page of this evening's paper. It was Julian Kane's son you saved, and that counts for something around here even if your rescue doesn't.'

'Oh Lord!' Lorna frowned. 'Look, I have to hurry to be on duty at the hospital at two.'

'Then by my guest. I can drive you to the hospital and we can talk on the way.'

Lorna sighed as she gained the impression that events were shaping beyond her control. Somewhere in the background, under the normal stream of everyday life, an unknown factor was operating on her behalf and she could sense it. She was faintly troubled by it because she had lived in obscurity for so long, in a rut that had been very private. But now it seemed that her past was being swept away precipitately and she mentally resigned herself as she was driven into town by the reporter.

SIX

By the time they reached the hospital Lorna had explained in great detail how she had saved Simon Kane from certain death. Sprague thanked her as she alighted from his car.

'I'll let you have some spare copies of the paper,' he promised. 'They'll come in handy if you ever start keeping a scrap book.'

'Thanks, but I'll want to live this down as quickly as possible,' she retorted.

He waved and drove off, and Lorna drew a deep breath and went into the hospital. She almost bumped into Jack Foster, who was waiting just inside the entrance, and when she looked into his face she saw that he was very serious.

'Is something wrong?' she demanded.

'I'll say there is.' He narrowed his eyes,

then smiled grimly. 'Who was that man who drove you here? Don't tell me you've got a secret lover, Lorna! I've been trying everything I know to get you to go out with me but you turn me down no matter what kind of an approach I make. I thought you were still mourning the death of your husband and son and that's why I didn't put too much pressure on you. Indeed, I thought that you were so deeply immersed in your grief that you would need expert help to get out of it. But it seems that I was sadly wrong in my diagnosis! You are a dark horse, Lorna Parry, and I want an accounting from you.'

'It certainly isn't what you think, Jack,' she replied, gazing at him in startled fashion, but her face cleared when he grinned.

'Don't look so worried,' he said. 'I know the local newshound, or I should know him, the times he's come into Casualty when I've been on duty there. I've heard all about your epic life-saving attempt this morning. Everyone in the hospital knows about it. Julian Kane is the most influential man around here, and when his son's life is saved by a local angel of mercy then everyone's got to know about it.'

Lorna suppressed a sigh. 'I'd better get up to the ward,' she said. 'I don't want to be late.'

'I'll walk up with you. There are one or two patients I need to talk about, but let's not talk shop until you're on duty. I want to ask you some personal questions. I want you to agree to going out with me one evening, and I won't take no for an answer any more.'

'I'm sorry, Jack, but I don't want to start something that might complicate my life.'

'Life! You call this living? You exist only for duty. I've never known anyone like you. Surely you weren't like this before your family died.'

'I'd rather you didn't keep bringing that up,' she said sharply. 'I'm trying to push it behind me and forget about it as much as possible.'

'Sorry.' He grimaced as they ascended the stairs to the upper wards. 'It must still be a tender subject. But you really ought to be getting out and about more and taking a fresh interest in life, Lorna. I have a great deal of feeling for you, and I'd give you an easy time.'

'I'm sure you would, and I'm sure you'd be good for me, but although I like you a great deal, Jack, I know there could never be anything serious between us. That's why I think it's better that we don't form a friendship. I wouldn't want any developments to complicate my life.'

'But you feel differently about Julian Kane!' He gazed into her startled eyes for a moment, then nodded slowly. 'Don't bother to deny it. I can see that I struck very close to the heart then, even if you're not aware of the fact yourself.'

'Now you're being absurd,' she said firmly. 'I didn't know he existed before yesterday. Oh, I'd heard of him. Who around here hasn't? But I'd never set eyes on him. He wasn't very pleasant to me either, when I met him, was he?'

'So what were you doing out at his place this morning?'

Lorna compressed her lips as she considered and they reached the top floor before she could answer.

'I usually drive out that way when I'm off duty. It's a beautiful area. The scenery around there has always been a favourite vista of mine.'

'But you were inside the grounds. You saved that child from a pool on the estate.'

'You sound disappointed, as if you're sorry I was on hand to save him,' Lorna countered, and it was his turn to look startled. But he shook his head, and Lorna placed a hand upon his arm. 'I don't want to fall out with you, Jack,' she said softly. 'So leave it be, will you?'

'All right.' He shrugged somewhat help-lessly and left her standing, striding away quickly, his shoulders stiff and his head held high.

Lorna gazed after him, and there was a pang in her breast as she considered. She had been aware for some time that he was attracted to her. She had noted his feelings intensifying over the months, but there had never been the slightest sense of reciprocation in her mind and she knew she was doing the right thing by consistently refusing to go out with him, aware that the slightest encouragement on her part would send him hopelessly head over heels in love with her.

She went on duty with her mind whirling under the sudden stresses that had fallen upon her, and was irritated by the congratulations bestowed upon her by patients and staff alike. But she went about her work relentlessly, trying to keep her concentration upon the more important issues. However as the afternoon began to wear away her thoughts turned to Julian Kane, and just before it was time for visitors to leave she saw him coming along the corridor towards her office.

Lorna found her heart was beating a trifle faster than normal as she led him into the office, and when they were seated at her desk she studied his set face. He was still rather pale, and she felt a wave of sympathy surge through her.

'How is Simon now?' she asked, trying to keep her voice steady. 'I checked on him as soon as I arrived on duty and learned that he is suffering no ill effects beyond shock.'

'I'm taking him home with me when I leave now,' he replied. He studied her face for a moment and she felt her cheeks begin to burn. 'What about you, Sister?'

'I'm fine,' she replied. 'I feel on top of the world. It gives one a nice feeling to save a life, after the shock of it has worn off.'

'I'm in your debt,' he said softly.

She shook her head. 'Not at all. It was a pleasure. It was the greatest thing I've ever done.'

'I can't believe that. You work here in the hospital. You must have saved a great number of lives in your time.' He caught his breath. 'When I think of the importance of your life and the way I've practically wasted mine I'm filled with a sense of shame.'

'From all accounts you've done pretty well in business,' she countered.

'I've been fortunate, and if I hadn't been in the position I was born to then no one would have missed the efforts I've made in this life. But it's different with you. There must be a number of people living today who owe their present health to you. Simon would be dead now if you hadn't happened along this morning. God! I break out into a sweat every time I think about it!'

'Well, put it out of your mind. That's the best thing to do. Simon didn't drown this morning and nothing can ever alter that.'

'That's the right attitude to hold, but I'm going to have nightmares for the rest of my life.'

'I suspect you're still badly shocked by the car accident, and this business of Simon has piled up rather high on top of you. I suggest you see my father and let him prescribe something for you.'

'I should have seen your father this

afternoon anyway, but what happened this morning drove it right out of my head.'

'I expect my mother told him what happened.' She explained about the newspaper reporter and he smiled.

'I rang the newspaper office,' he admitted, 'I have shares in the company, and I want you to get full credit and recognition for what you did.'

'You shouldn't have done that. I don't like the limelight.' She glanced reluctantly at her watch, aware that she did not have much time, and he saw her action and immediately arose to his feet.

'I haven't any right to keep you when you're so busy,' he said. 'Simon has been asking a lot of questions about you. I've promised him that I'd get you to spend some time with us during the week-end. It's Saturday tomorrow and I know you're off duty. Have you made any arrangements?'

'I haven't. I never do.' She spoke quietly, thinking of the lonely days she had known.

'Good. Shall I send my car for you at

about ten-thirty in the morning? I'm sure you'd like to look around the Manor. It's a wonderful old place, if you like that sort of thing.'

'Fine.' She nodded and smiled. 'I'll look forward to seeing Simon tomorrow.'

'I'll tell him he'll be able to see you. But I hope he won't cause any trouble in your life. You lost a son of your own who would have been about Simon's age, didn't you?'

'Yes.' She sighed heavily, and for a moment the old familiar cloud presented itself in her mind, but almost as quickly it vanished, and she felt little more than a shadow of the pain she used to know.

'Forgive me if you still can't talk about it,' he continued. 'But that's the best medicine in the world, you know.' He held out his hand and Lorna grasped it, tingling at their contact. His grip was strong, and she clenched her teeth as an undefinable pang cut through her breast. But her smile never faltered.

'Until tomorrow then,' she said.

'I think I'm looking forward to the change your company will bring.' He was smiling broadly. 'Poor Simon has had a lonely life until now. I've got to do something to make it up to him. At the moment he wants to see you, and I've managed to persuade you to visit with us. That's a great start.'

'It's been a long time since I went out anywhere,' she admitted.

After he had departed she sat at the desk thinking about the situation, and it wasn't until one of the nurses appeared to ask her a question that she managed to drag her thoughts from her personal matters and return to duty. Then time seemed to run riot and the rest of her shift whirled by. She felt caught up in events which were larger than life. Whenever she thought of the next day and all the promise it seemed to hold she could scarcely believe that it had come about. She was half afraid that she would suddenly awaken to find that it had all been a strange dream.

Just before six she was surprised when

Matron walked into her office, and she put down her pen and arose to greet her superior. Mrs Marlowe was carrying an evening paper, and she paused in front of Lorna, tall and slender, with dark eyes that were sparkling with pleasure.

'I don't want to stop you, Sister,' she said, 'but I just had to come along and congratulate you on the wonderful thing you did this morning.'

'Thank you, Matron.' Lorna could not help but glance at the newspaper in Matron's hand, and gasped when she saw the headlines boldly displayed.

Matron handed the paper to her, and Lorna read the glowing account of the rescue. There was even a photograph of her gazing up from the printed page, and she guessed that the reporter had returned to her home and asked for a snapshot.

'There was no need for all this,' she said awkwardly. 'Anyone in a similar situation would have done the same thing, Matron.'

'But it was you there on the spot, and I'm

very pleased that the rescue was successful. You're to be highly commended, Sister, and no doubt the proper authorities will decide if your act of bravery should receive the recognition it so richly deserves.'

Lorna was breathing heavily with excitement by the time Matron departed, and she had to make an effort to retain a firm grip upon her emotions. Then Jack Foster appeared, and he was carrying several copies of the evening edition.

'Sprague asked me to pass these on to you,' he said abruptly. 'Quite a heroine, aren't you? What did Kane want with you when he was up here?'

'He thanked me for what I'd done. It's only natural that he should, don't you think? It was his only son I saved.'

'Perhaps you're making too much of that fact,' Foster said.

'What do you mean?' Lorna took a firm grip upon her feelings as she studied his intent face.

'I mean that you may be letting all this

publicity and glory sweep you off your feet. I've heard that you're going to Kane's place for the week-end.'

'Where did you hear that? How could you have learned of it?' Lorna was startled.

'Not via the usual channels, I assure you.' He smiled bitterly. 'I happen to know Isobel Garvin very well and she telephoned me this afternoon.'

'Really! I don't see what concern it is of hers!' Lorna could feel her cheeks burning.

'Perhaps it concerns her more than you realize.' He leaned forward and gazed into Lorna's eyes. She wished she could turn away from him to conceal her expression, certain that it was betraying her. But his manner and words held her attention. 'You don't know what you're letting yourself in for, Lorna. There was a considerable amount of scandal about the death of Mrs Kane. Since then Julian Kane has been indulging himself with the fair sex. I'd hate to see you get caught up in that kind of thing. You're not his type, and you'd fall pretty hard if he started working his wiles upon you.'

'Thank you for your concern,' she retorted, and suddenly there was anger boiling inside her. 'But you have no right to take this attitude. It's certainly none of your business what I do off duty and away from the hospital. I think you over-estimate our friendship if you presume to advise me on a situation that certainly doesn't exist and never seems likely to.'

'All right.' He lifted his hands placatingly. 'I'm just giving you a friendly warning, that's all. I am on your side, remember. Don't go into this with stars in your eyes, that's all I ask. From what Isobel Garvin told me, she's expecting Kane to ask her to marry him. I'm sure you wouldn't want to put your foot in the middle of that situation, would you?'

Lorna stared at him, breathing hard, trying mentally to refute the statement he had made. But despite her efforts to remain calm she was aware that there was a sinking sensation in her mind and her spirits were suddenly down at zero. She felt utterly deflated, but made an effort to keep the obvious signs of it out of her expression.

'It doesn't really concern me about Mr Kane's personal life,' she said. 'I'm interested only in Simon. He does remind me of my son, Jack, and I wouldn't be human if I didn't notice the fact. But I can take care of myself.'

'I'm wondering whether you can,' he retorted. 'I don't like this, Lorna.'

He departed then, and she gazed at the door while reflecting upon his words. Then her thoughts turned inwards upon her own attitude and she found herself wondering exactly what her hopes and intentions were. She could not deny that she was un-accountably interested in Simon Kane, but that was as far as her mind would take her. She had no interest in Julian Kane. Her sense of grief was such that it precluded her from forming an attachment for anyone.

When she went off duty at ten that night

she was tired and depressed. A figure startled her by appearing from the shadows around the main gate, and she caught her breath when she recognised Julian Kane. His deep voice came at her like a caress.

'Hello, Sister. I was in the area and knew you finished at ten. I promised Simon before I came out that I'd look you up. He picked these for you.'

He held out a small bunch of wild flowers, smiling, his teeth gleaming, and Lorna sighed deeply as she accepted them.

'Primroses and violets,' she said softly. 'How sweet!'

'Off the estate,' he continued. 'I took Simon for a stroll after tea and he insisted on sending them to you.'

'They're beautiful.' Lorna raised the posy and sniffed delicately, catching the fragrant perfume of the violets, and some intangible chord seemed to vibrate in her mind as she breathed deeply. 'Thank him for me, won't you? It was very thoughtful of him.'

'You'll be able to thank him yourself

tomorrow morning,' he remarked. 'May I drive you home now? You didn't come in your car, did you?'

'I never come to the hospital by car,' she replied. 'Thank you. A lift will save me the bother of having to wait for a bus.'

'This way then.' He moved to the left, and as Lorna followed she heard footsteps in the hospital yard. The next moment the tall figure of Jack Foster loomed up and she experienced a momentary pang of worry.

'Goodnight, Lorna,' Forster called, turning to the right and striding off.

'Goodnight,' she responded, her tone unsteady.

Kane was driving a large grey Jaguar, and he opened the door for her, smiling as their gazes met. Lorna slid into the front passenger seat and sat holding the posy while he went around the car and slid in behind the wheel. There he paused and looked at her.

'I can't really believe this is happening,' he commented.

'Why not?' She studied his face intently, wondering about Jack Foster's words about the situation surrounding Julian Kane. But there was no expression on Kane's face.

'I keep thinking of what happened this morning. You saved Simon's life. I didn't know you existed until yesterday, and when I first set eyes upon you I told myself that you were a hard woman. It just shows how wrong a man can be.'

'Really?' She was intrigued, and continued watching his face as he started the car. 'You were judging me by my appearance, no doubt. What was there about me that gave you the impression I was hard?'

'Your expression. It looked hard. But that was only a first impression. When I looked at you later I could see that what I thought was harshness was merely a barrier you had erected against the rest of the world.'

'Surely it doesn't show that plainly!' There was shock in her voice and he smiled grimly as he cast a glance at her.

'No. It wouldn't show to anyone who

hasn't experienced the self-same thing. But I've been through that particular hell and can recognise all the signs.'

'I think I've begun to jerk myself out of that particular rut,' She declared, sighing and trying to relax. 'It's been three years.'

'I know. I've learned quite a lot about you since yesterday.' He suppressed a sigh, and was silent for a moment as he drove towards the outskirts of the town.

Lorna remained stiff and motionless at his side, trying to analyse her thoughts. Was there any truth in what Foster had said? Was she attracted to this handsome man and pretended that the boy was the real cause? But he was a stranger and she had never been quick to make friends let alone permit herself to be attracted to anyone.

All too soon they reached her home and he brought the car to a halt in front of the house.

'I assume that you always go straight home when you get off duty,' he commented.

'I'm usually ready to put up my feet by the

time I've finished a shift at the hospital,' she replied.

'I can well imagine. The experiences of the past two days have certainly opened my eyes. I didn't know what a nurse's life consisted of.'

Lorna listened intently to the sound of his voice, feeling a great reluctance to leave him. He twisted to face her, the fingers of his right hand tapping idly upon the steering wheel. A little light filtered into the vehicle from the windows of the lounge, and she caught her breath as she fought down the unfamiliar emotions that welled up inside her like water in a mountain spring.

'Simon has already made a lot of plans for this week-end,' he continued, gazing at her in a way that seemed to disconcert her. She was trying to tell herself that Isobel Garvin was hoping to become the second Mrs Kane, but the fact would not drive through her hammering emotion. 'You'll tell me if what is planned turns out to be too strenuous for you, will you not?'

'I have the feeling that I shall thoroughly enjoy myself,' she replied steadily, and a nervous sigh gusted through her. 'I have taken quite a liking to your son, Mr Kane, and I'd like to see him again.'

'He's feeling the same way about you. Of course, he's missing his mother. But don't think that I'm trying to bring you two together because of that. Yet you could help each other, if I understand the situation correctly. Simon was never one to make friends easily. Ever since he was a baby he found it difficult to take to people. That's one of the reasons why I wanted your father to see him. I don't want him to grow up anti-social.'

'I'll be able to tell you a great deal about him by the time the week-end is over,' said Lorna, ignoring the small voice in her mind that was protesting strongly. She was suddenly feeling afraid because her emotions seemed to be slipping from out of her control and she had never permitted them so much laxity. But she knew that if she were not careful the situation could get out of control, and this was what Jack and her mother had warned her about.

SEVEN

When she finally got to bed that night,
Lorna found it very difficult to sleep, but
eventually she did drop off and slept
heavily, to awaken next morning just before
eight. Glancing anxiously towards the
window, she was pleased to see sunlight
streaming into the room. It was going to be
a fine day. She arose and began to prepare
for her visit to Cairn Manor, and was soon
ready to leave. But she controlled her impatience and sat with her mother at the
breakfast table. There was a leaping of
pleasure in her breast and she felt like a
school-girl about to embark upon some
long-awaited treat.

Precisely at ten-thirty a car pulled up in
front of the house, and Lorna crossed to the
window in her eagerness to see who had

called for her. Julian Kane was driving his Jaguar and Simon was seated in the back. Mrs Parry came to Lorna's side and gazed with undisguised interest at the car and its occupants, but drew back when Julian alighted from the car and approached the front door.

'I'll go straight out, Mother,' Lorna said hurriedly. 'I don't know where we're going or what time I shall get back, so you'd better expect me when you see me.'

'Have a nice time, dear. You deserve it,' declared Mrs Parry, and Lorna hugged her and turned quickly to answer the door as the bell rang.

She was breathless as she gazed into Julian's smiling face, and there was quick admiration in his eyes as he looked her over. She was wearing a pink two-piece suit with a pale silk blouse underneath, and knew her eyes were glistening, her face showing pleasure.

'We're right on time and you're ready and waiting,' he said easily. 'I expect it's your nursing training that makes you so punctual, eh?'

'I expect so,' she replied, and looked towards the car, feeling a little bit overwhelmed by her feelings and his nearness. 'How is Simon this morning?'

'Fine, and filled with excitement at the prospect of having a day out.'

'I must confess that I feel exactly the same,' she admitted.

'You haven't been far in the past three years, so I've heard,' he retorted, taking her arm and leading her towards the big car.

Lorna trembled at their contact, and it was all she could do to prevent a perceptible shudder tearing through her. But he did not seem to be aware of her reaction and opened the front passenger door for her. When she was seated, Lorna turned to look at Simon, who was gazing shyly at her, a faint smile upon his lips.

'Hello, Simon,' she greeted cheerfully. 'How are you this morning? It's very kind of you to invite me out like this. You must have known that I don't go out much when I'm not at the hospital.'

'I'm glad you're coming with us. I never go out with Daddy, so we're both lucky.'

'You're luckier than most, Simon,' commented Julian getting into the car. 'If it wasn't for Sister Parry you wouldn't be here now.'

'I think we should try to forget all about that,' cut in Lorna. 'I'm sure Simon doesn't want to be reminded of it, and I feel embarrassed at the fuss that was kicked up afterwards.'

'I'm glad I nearly drowned,' said Simon. 'If I hadn't then you wouldn't have been able to save me and we wouldn't be out like this today.'

'I like the simplicity of a child's mind,' commented Julian, starting the car.

But Simon was deadly serious and his eyes glinted as he looked at Lorna.

'I wish you could take care of me instead of Miss Isobel. You know more than she does. You saved my life.'

Lorna smiled, although she did not know how to answer, and Julian stepped into the breach that seemed to yawn before her.

'Well,' he said cheerfully. 'We have all day before us. Where shall we go? You've been trying to make up your mind ever since you awakened this morning, Simon. Have you reached a decision yet?'

'It's Sister Parry's day out too. Let's do what she wants,' said the boy.

'I'm sure you've given more thought to it than I have,' countered Lorna. 'What would you really like to do, Simon?' She could feel emotion tugging at her inside, for half-forgotten memories of her own dead son returned to her mind.

'I'd like to look at a castle, then walk along a beach,' Simon said. 'Isobel has been promising to take me but never does.'

'That's settled then.' Julian set the car in motion. 'Mrs Heywood has packed a tremendous picnic basket. I think I know just the place you'd like, Simon, so hold tight and we'll be off.'

Lorna mentally crossed her fingers as they departed, hoping that the day would prove to be all that it was promising. She soon discovered that she was enjoying herself immensely, and the sunny hours slipped away all too quickly. They visited a castle and then went on to the sea-side, where they spent most of the afternoon running on the sands or looking for crabs and shellfish in the pools amongst the rocks on the shore.

Simon enjoyed himself, his shrill voice echoing repeatedly as he called or laughed, and Lorna found herself completely absorbed with the boy. Long before the day drew to a close they were the best of friends, and a bond seemed to have grown between them by the time they returned to the car and Julian decided they had to start the return trip.

'I want to sit with you, Lorna,' Simon said as they got into the car. They had come naturally to first-name terms, and he snuggled himself on Lorna's lap, falling asleep before they had covered a mile, his head resting on her shoulder.

They were mainly silent on the drive back to Cairn Manor, and Lorna found herself dozing, musing over the happy events of the day. She glanced at Julian, saw that he was humming to himself, his face showing a relaxed expression, and caught herself up for a moment, a pang of wonder striking through her, at being in this car with a man who was practically a stranger.

But he wasn't a stranger! The knowledge came jolting into her mind. She stiffened for a few moments, gazing ahead, letting her mind have full sway. He had never seemed like a stranger, not even when she had first set eyes upon him. Simon too! She felt as if she had always known him.

Her mind hadn't once slipped into the black rut of grief that had occupied it during the recent years. Thinking of her loss now, she knew that none of the old anguish was present, and guessed that at last the painful memories had taken their rightful place in the background where they belonged.

As they were nearing Rossglen, Julian glanced sideways at her, and Lorna looked at him, attracted by his movement.

'I thought you'd dropped off,' he commented softly. 'That's why I didn't speak.'

'No,' she said quietly, gazing up at the red-gold sunset over the distant mountains. The sky seemed ablaze, glorying in its crimson splendour, and all the tiny white clouds were limned with vivid fire. Strange sensations passed through her. 'I've been thinking,' she added.

'I'm marvelling at the way Simon has taken to you. I've never seen him so animated before, not even when his mother was alive. For myself, I've really enjoyed today, and I hope you haven't been bored by the simplicity of our pleasure.'

'Bored? I can't remember the last time I enjoyed myself so much. It's been heavenly.'

'Then there's hope that when I ask you to give us your company tomorrow you'll say yes?'

She glanced at him, and his dark eyes were

steady as they flickered to look at her before returning to watch the road ahead.

'A pony is being delivered in the morning,' he went on. 'I've been promising Simon one for a long time, and I'd like to have you around when he sees it. Do you know anything about ponies?'

'I had one as a girl.' Lorna's blue eyes glistened as she recalled. 'It was a pretty little white one, and she was so knowing I always thought she was human. I'm an only child, you know, and that's why I feel for Simon, because I know how lonely he must be at times.'

'Only he's been far lonelier than you. His mother is dead and his father has never found much time for him. But I expect you received all the love in the world from both your parents. You certainly appear to be a person who had a well-balanced childhood.'

Lorna nodded slowly, and again felt emotion rising inside her. She glanced down at the dark head of the sleeping child and, for a moment, knew the intangible longings of a mother for her son. She firmed her lips and gazed ahead. Rossglen lay in the distance and they were approaching it much too rapidly for her. Then Simon stirred and awakened, and Lorna hugged him instinctively.

'We're almost home,' she said quietly, and the child's hands clutched at her arms.

'I don't want to go home yet,' he said. 'The time has gone too quickly.'

'But it's getting dark, and near to your bed-time,' said Julian. 'There's always tomorrow, Simon.'

'Will you be coming out with us again tomorrow, Lorna,' the boy asked.

'I haven't been asked yet,' she responded, her eyes alive with animation.

'Simon's just asked you,' put in Julian, keeping his eyes on the road ahead.

'Please!' insisted Simon.

'If I haven't been a nuisance today then I'll be happy to share your company tomorrow.' Lorna stilled her breathing for a moment, and when she saw the relief which showed in Simon's eyes she knew that no matter what came up in the future, she would never do anything to hurt the boy.

'That's settled then.' There was a decisive note in Julian's voice. 'We'd better start making arrangements now, because you'll be going to bed as soon as we reach home, Simon.'

'We could pick up Lorna tomorrow like we did today,' Simon suggested.

'That sounds like a good idea.' Lorna nodded. 'I'll be ready at the same time, if you like.'

'Perhaps thirty minutes earlier,' Julian said. 'I have a reason for suggesting it.'

'All right. I'll be ready at ten.'

'What shall we do tomorrow?' Simon demanded excitedly.

'I think we'll leave that part of the arrangements until the morning,' replied Julian.

Lorna leaned back in her seat and tried to stop all worries concerning the future from invading her mind. There was nothing that could go wrong. She was convinced of that.

All she was interested in was Simon's welfare, but when she glanced sideways at Julian's intent face she felt a rising tide of awareness and emotion sweeping through her.

Suddenly she found herself longing to reach out and touch his lean, strong hands on the steering wheel, to press her fingers against his firm chin, and she caught her breath, shocked by the power of that impulsive desire. She clenched her teeth and firmed her lips, trying to analyse the emotion, and it seemed to rise to fever heat, moving her with its intensity. She began to wonder what it would be like to feel his arms around her, his mouth against hers, and she shivered inside, trembling with unexpected fervour.

She had been in his company all day and he was the first man in three years with whom she had spent any time. Their proximity was having a natural effect upon her, and as she realized it she closed her eyes and tried to fight down the knowledge that it would be all too easy to fall in love with him.

She hardly heard Simon's chatter as they covered the last miles to Cairn Manor, and when they finally turned into the driveway and went on to the rambling old house, Lorna felt a pang of regret because the day had come to an end.

'Aren't we taking Lorna home first?' Simon demanded as Julian brought the car to a standstill in front of the house.

'Lorna doesn't have to go to bed as early as you, young man,' Julian replied. 'And I thought you might like to have her put you to bed. You're going to see her again tomorrow, but if we don't give her some time without you then she might get tired of being around us and not come again.'

'You will want to see us again, won't you, Lorna?' There was sudden anxiety in the boy's voice, and Lorna smiled.

'You need never worry that I'll suddenly not come again,' she promised. 'The only time I'll stop coming is when you tell me that you're tired of me.'

'That will never be!' The boy clung to her as they alighted from the car. 'Tell her, Daddy, that we want her to keep seeing us.'

'She knows that by now, I imagine,' Julian replied steadily, and Lorna drew a long breath as they ascended the steps to the front door and entered the house.

She put Simon to bed, and they had more fun before the boy finally settled down. Julian bent and kissed his son's cheek, and Simon held out his hands to Lorna, who went forward and embraced him. Simon kissed her fervently, and the touch of his innocent mouth reminded her of the horror of the previous day down at the pool. Shivers darted through her and she cringed inwardly.

'Goodnight, Simon,' she whispered. 'I'll expect you to come for me in the morning.'

'We won't forget,' came the excited reply, and the boy settled himself in the bed and closed his eyes. 'I'll pray for tomorrow to come quickly, shall I?'

'I'll do the same,' Lorna promised.

Julian took her arm as they tiptoed from the room, and when he had closed the bedroom door he paused in the dim corridor and looked down at Lorna. She studied his face, wondering what was passing through his mind, and saw him shake his head, as if his thoughts were muddled.

'I'll certainly be in your debt for the rest of my life,' he said quietly. 'You've done wonders with that boy today.'

'You owe me nothing. I'm finding that being in Simon's company has also helped me. I think we'll break even on this.'

He nodded and took her arm again, leading her towards the stairs, and Lorna shivered at his touch.

'I can't decide what effect you're having on me,' he went on as they descended the stairs. 'I've never met a girl quite like you, Lorna.'

'What's so different about me?' she demanded, trying to keep her tone casual.

'You're so selfless that it shines out of your eyes. There aren't many women who would have given up so much of their limited spare time for a child.'

'But I like Simon, and it was pure pleasure, not duty.'

He led her into the large drawing room. 'Are you in a hurry to go home?' he asked, and she shook her head, unable to trust herself to speak because his nearness seemed to make her tongue-tied. Her mouth was dry, her throat constricted, and she had to make an effort to say something.

'No,' she finally managed. 'But you've had a long day, and I'm sure you haven't quite recovered from the ill effects of your accident.'

'Or the shock of almost losing Simon,' he added.

The door of the room was opened and Isobel Garvin appeared. She paused on the threshold and stared at them, her eyes narrowing when she saw Lorna.

'I'm sorry,' she said harshly. 'I wasn't

aware of your return.'

'It's all right,' replied Julian. 'I'm about to drive Lorna home.'

It was the first time he had used her name directly that day, and Lorna fought to keep her face expressionless as she heard it on his lips. But she saw a sneer on Isobel's face as the girl turned and departed. A silence developed which seemed a trifle awkward, and it was the first time that such a condition had arisen between them.

'Shall I get you a drink?' Julian asked.

'No thank you. Perhaps I had better be going if I'm to spend tomorrow with you and Simon.'

'Are you sure you want to?' He arose and faced her as she stood up, and Lorna found herself standing very close to him and gazing into his eyes.

'Yes.' Her voice was uneven. She saw him nod, and suddenly his eyes were filled with an expression which seemed to touch a chord in her soul. She caught her breath, knowing that his nearness during the day

157

had been subconsciously tormenting her, and suddenly he was placing his hands upon her shoulders and coming even closer.

'I can understand why Simon is so taken up with you,' he said huskily. 'You've even had a strange effect upon me, Lorna, and I can't explain it. Something inside me has been made to sit up and take notice. It could be that I'm lonely. My wife has been dead three years. I don't know what's behind it, but I do know that if I never saw you again I'd find life even worse than it was before I met you.'

She could only gaze at him, her lips compressed, and there was an ache in her breast. But his words only added to the fire that seemed to burn within her, and she blinked because emotion was stinging her eyes. He was taut and stiff before her, gazing into her face with a worried frown upon his handsome face, his dark eyes glistening. But when she remained silent his tension suddenly escaped and his shoulders sagged.

'I'm sorry,' he said. 'This is a fine way to

thank you for giving so much of your time to my child. But I had to say it because I'm certain that if I see you again I'm going to fall head over heels in love with you. I wouldn't want to complicate your life, especially after the way you've helped me. Perhaps I'd better take you home and forget all about you.'

'No!' She gulped to get rid of the clogging sensation that filled her. There was only one clear thought in her mind at that moment. She wanted to see him again! After today she did not want to go back to her existence of all duty and no pleasure. He and his son had opened her eyes to the emptiness of her life. It was all very well devoting oneself to the care of the sick, but one was entitled to a little pleasure and now she was afraid he would make the decision that would cut them off from each other. 'Oh no,' she said quietly. 'Can't you see? Everything you said about yourself also applies to me. It was as if you were talking about my feelings and not your own.'

His face expressed surprise, and a flash of hope glinted in his brown eyes. He breathed deeply and his hands tightened upon her slim shoulders.

'Could it possibly be?' he whispered, then slowly shook his head. 'I wouldn't dare to hope that you could be attracted to me. It seems the attraction was all on our side. Simon took an instant liking to you, and I've had the devil of a job finding someone who suited him. His present governess is on holiday at the moment because of trouble, and she's probably looking for another post. Isobel, my secretary, has been taking care of him while attempting to carry out her other duties, but he's not too keen on her, although she seems to have a knack of handling him. But you're a different kettle of fish! I've never known him to take such a shine to anyone before.'

The mention of Isobel Garvin sent a pang through Lorna but she pushed it to the background. Nothing else seemed to matter at that moment. There were only two of them together in a harsh world, and Lorna sensed that whatever strange force was attracting them, it would not be content until they had discovered the full extent of their feelings.

'I've been in a torment all day,' he confessed in husky tones. 'I have never felt like this before. I wanted to reach out and touch you, but I was afraid you might misunderstand. But if you feel the same way about me then you must understand.'

'I understand.' She nodded slowly, recalling her emotions in the car when she had resisted the urge to touch him. 'I don't know what's pushing me, but I can accept it.'

The next moment she was in his arms, and he groaned softly as they embraced. She could feel, as if in a dream, his warm breath upon her cheek, and emotion set her mind aflame with a fire that would never be extinguished. She clung to him, casting aside the miseries and doubts of the past, and they swayed in the power of their passions.

When he kissed her, Lorna was torn with a series of tremors, and she remotely accepted that this was the work of Destiny. A quirk of fate had brought them together and in the short time since their meeting they had discovered that each held the power to help the other. The only dark thought in her mind at that poignant moment was of the future and what it might hold for them. Were they destined to find happiness or were they doomed to abject disappointment, to a return to their past grief? She did not know or care at the moment, but she mentally crossed her fingers and hoped for the best.

EIGHT

Sunday morning found Lorna in an unusual mood. She awoke with a song in her heart, and it was all she could do to compose herself before appearing at the breakfast table with her parents. She was impatient to see Julian again, and her mouth still seemed to burn with a strange intensity as she recalled the power of his kisses.

'You're perky this morning,' observed Mrs Parry.

'Why not?' Lorna was in the act of leaving the room, afraid of being asked too many questions about the previous day. 'This is my week-end off duty and the weather is perfect.'

'You're not sickening for something, are you?' her father demanded, glancing up from newspaper. 'I haven't heard that tone

163

in your voice for a long time.'

Lorna smiled and departed quickly, pausing to reopen the door and call to her mother.

'I shall be collected at ten this morning and I won't be home all day.'

'Have a nice time, dear,' Mrs Parry called after her.

But there were butterflies at work inside Lorna as the appointed hour approached. She began to feel anticipation doing its own special work in her mind, and wondered if she would feel embarrassed when she saw Julian again, after the passion that had built up between them the previous evening.

However her pleasure at seeing him again drove all thoughts of the previous day from her mind as she hurried out to the car when it drew up in front of the house. She saw Simon's smiling face at a window and there was a broad grin on Julian's features as he alighted and came towards her.

'Hello,' he greeted softly. 'How are you feeling this morning?'

164

'Fine,' she responded. 'Very well.'

For a moment their gazes met and held, and Lorna felt her breath catching in her throat. She moistened her lips, her mind working fast, telling her that what passed between them the day before had been the result of genuine emotion and not a convulsive clutching at some elusive, intangible dream that each desired.

'Come on, Lorna,' Simon called from the car, and there was a tinge of excitement in his tone. 'Daddy says we're going straight back home, and there's a surprise waiting for me.'

They got into the car and departed, and when Lorna glanced back at the house she caught a glimpse of her mother's face peering from a window. She smiled wryly. She could not tell if she was doing the right thing. Life itself was a gamble and one had to make a number of mistakes and take a great many things on trust. She was determined not to question this situation too closely, or to expect too much from it. She was deriving great pleasure from it, and that was all that mattered.

Simon was overjoyed to be in her company again, and elated by the promise of a surprise. The boy's pleasure knew no bounds when they reached Cairn Manor and went to the stables at the rear, where a black pony was being unloaded from a horsebox. Simon went into a paroxysm of delight, and, when he had managed to control his emotions somewhat, they spent the rest of the morning teaching him how to sit a saddle and how to care for the animal.

The day passed very quickly. They had lunch together on the grey stone terrace, and laughter and happy chatter sounded all the time. During the afternoon Simon had a nap, and Julian showed Lorna over the large house. After tea they went for a short walk in the grounds, and then, all too soon, it was time for Simon to go to bed.

Lorna found herself suffering pangs of disappointment as she entered the boy's bedroom, and Simon clung to her as they kissed goodnight. The boy looked at Julian, who remained in the background.

'Thank you for the pony, Daddy,' he said sleepily. 'And thank you for showing me how to ride, Lorna. I've never had such a happy day. Shall I see you tomorrow?'

'I'm on duty at six in the morning,' said Lorna. 'I finish at two in the afternoon.'

'I have school lessons tomorrow, but they finish early. Shall we see Lorna tomorrow evening, Daddy?'

'I'll work out something with her,' Julian replied gravely, and Simon settled himself to sleep.

When they left the room, Lorna found herself brimming with emotion, and turned to Julian as he slid a hand under her elbow.

'I don't know who has been the more excited today,' he said, 'you or Simon.'

'It's been a wonderful day.' She sighed deeply. 'And what about you? Have you enjoyed yourself?' She could see pleasure in his eyes, and his face proclaimed that he had derived benefit from the week-end. He was no longer pale and tense.

He nodded slowly. 'The last two days have been a real tonic. It seems to me as if we've been caught up in a dream, but tomorrow reality returns, doesn't it? You have to go back on duty and Simon returns to his schooling. I shall do nothing in business, but there's no fun in being alone. I'd like to take you out, Lorna. Just the two of us for once, so we can discuss the situation which seems to have risen.'

'I'd like that myself,' she responded.

'Tomorrow evening then?' There was eagerness in his voice.

'What about Simon?'

'We'll think of something. He won't mind us going off alone.'

'I started out with the intention of doing what I could to relieve Simon's loneliness,' she said thoughtfully. 'Now, after only two days, we're trying to make excuses to get away from him.'

'If you can give a rational explanation why I should be feeling this way then I'll be pleased to hear it,' he countered. 'I'm out of my depth. I don't know what to think any more. I've never been hit like this.'

'And the strange thing is that I feel exactly the same.' Lorna shook her head, filled with a sense of wonder. 'I asked myself the same questions last night and finally decided it would be better not to look ahead. I don't want to know why. I'm just content that it is happening.'

'Is it a kind of madness?' he demanded. 'Shall we suddenly come to our senses to find that we've hurt each other?'

'Don't let us think about it,' she begged, suddenly apprehensive.

He nodded and took her into his arms, and Lorna closed her eyes and uttered a silent prayer for the future.

From then on life seemed to accelerate, and she found herself going on duty, existing through the long hours at the hospital, then hurrying home to get out of uniform and meet Julian and Simon. They set a pattern to which they adhered, and time meant nothing and there was no opportunity of expanding generally because they kept to themselves and enjoyed their own company.

Lorna did not realize that changes were sneaking upon her. The days went by and time lengthened into weeks, then a month, and the habits into which they settled seemed to promise more than they could ever have hoped for.

She spent every available minute at Cairn Manor, being alone with Julian when Simon was doing his lessons. The boy seemed to have changed character since Lorna's advent into his life, and tolerated his governess now. But being alone with Julian meant sharing his company around the estate and gaining a peace of mind she had never thought possible. The past was irrevocably buried under a host of new and wonderful emotions and sensations that came pouring into her life, and she began to find it difficult to remember with any clarity the grim days when she had been bowed under the weight of grief.

Julian seemed to blossom with their friendship, and she discovered quite a number of points about him that surprised her. He was gentle and quiet, given to a seriousness which he could not overpower at times, but he was always responsive to her, aware of her feelings and showing consideration in every way.

Lorna began to wonder exactly what were her feelings towards him, but when she questioned herself upon that delicate subject, which was often, there seemed to be no clear answer. She was emotionally entangled with Julian and Simon, but could not classify what kind of emotion was involved, although there were certain pointers which could not be ignored. Whenever she was on duty or away from Julian she longed for the time when she would be free to go with him, and while she was in his company there was nothing else in the world that could measure up to the attraction he held for her. Slowly, he became the centre of her thoughts, and, slowly, she came to realize that she was in love with him. He and his son had filled the void in her heart left by the tragedy that had robbed her of a family.

But there were times when she found Julian tense and grim, and no amount of tactful questioning could draw him into an admission of trouble. She worried about his health, but he was obviously very well, and she tried to dismiss her dark forebodings with an explanation that he was still concerned about his own past, that it might take him longer to recover from it than it had taken her.

The week-ends were best, she discovered. With Simon, they went around the estate, carefree and very happy. On one afternoon some six weeks after first meeting, they took Simon for a walk across the moors, and when they were tired they sat down while the boy blithely chased butterflies.

'I've been thinking very seriously about you for some time now, Lorna,' remarked

Julian, and she looked at him intently, afraid that he was going to tell her their wonderful association must come to an end. 'There seems to be so much that needs to be said that I just don't know where to begin. I've noticed in your eyes these past weeks a sense of awareness that surely means you're in love with me.'

She opened her mouth to comment but no words came into her mind, and she turned her head and looked at the boyish figure of his son running hither and thither through the heather. When she returned her gaze to him she saw that he was regarding her closely.

'You've taken the place of Simon's mother, you know,' he went on slowly.

'I was aware of that at the outset. It was inevitable.' Lorna looked at him in sudden fear. What was he leading up to? Was he going to tell her that their association must now come to an end?

'I'm happy about that,' he said softly. 'You've changed Simon's life completely,

Lorna, and mine. You've come to mean a great deal to my son, and, more to the point, you've filled a deep void in my heart. My marriage was burdened with mistakes, and perhaps the biggest mistake of all was picking the wrong woman to begin with. When my wife died I didn't grieve for her in the way you must have grieved the loss of your husband and son. I wasn't in love with her for a long time before she died. We were opposites, and only a fool would have married under those circumstances. I was a fool, and because of that I'm afraid of making another mistake. I keep telling myself that you're right for me. I know you're right for Simon because he keeps telling me so in no uncertain terms. But I can't choose a wife because she happens to be right for my motherless son! I've got to pick someone I can love, someone who loves me.'

Lorna watched his serious face with steady gaze and her heart ached for him as she recognised the problems.

'I have the feeling that I do love you, Lorna, but I don't know how to make sure. I dare not take a chance that what I might think is love is merely appreciation for what you've done for Simon. In the very first place you saved his life. I've got to be fair to you. I've got to know what really is in my mind, because another mistake would make you unhappy too, and that's the last thing in the world I want.'

'I understand,' she said softly. 'There's no hurry for any decision, Julian. I am in love with you. Since I met you I've become happy. I didn't think such happiness could be possible after what happened. But there's no urgency in this for us, is there?'

'None at all, on the face of it. That's what makes you such a gem, Lorna. You understand so well.' He paused, and for a moment there was a sense of brooding in his expression. 'But it will not all be plain sailing, I fear.'

She did not question his words for she was aware that he could not answer. But she fancied that she understood, and later, when she went to the hospital on night duty, she applied herself furiously to her work because she had been guilty of letting her personal life loom up larger than duty. But her mind was clear and she felt on top of the world. Never had events gone along so well.

Jack Foster was the surgeon on duty, and Lorna was surprised when he entered her office just after one in the morning. He paused in the doorway, startling her with his silent approach, and she looked up at him quickly.

'You startled me!' she accused, putting down her pen and sighing.

'Any chance of some coffee?' he demanded, sitting down in the chair beside her desk. 'I know you sometimes make a cup during the night. I've got an Emergency Op coming in.'

'Certainly. It won't take a couple of minutes.' She glanced at her watch as she arose from the desk. 'I have some time to spare and I fancy a cup myself. Let's go along to the kitchen, shall we?'

They walked along the silent corridor to the small kitchen, and Lorna made the coffee. Foster sat down on a corner of the table, swinging one leg, his face showing that he was extremely thoughtful. Since their serious talk about Julian there had been little contact between them, and Lorna knew he was still angered by the way she had told him to stay out of her affairs. He had admitted to knowing Isobel Garvin very well, and she suspected that the secretary was keeping him informed of the situation developing at Cairn Manor. She felt a pang cut her as she regarded his pensive face, and realized that during the six weeks she had been seeing Julian and Simon she had not given any thought to other matters around her. She had come to the hospital, done her duty, and departed quickly. But now she recalled that Foster had admitted more than once to being in love with her, and when she imagined what his feelings must be like her conscience pricked her.

'What's the trouble, Jack?' she asked as she handed him a cup of coffee. 'You look as if you've just caught a contagious disease.'

'You're not interested in other people's problems any more,' he retorted, smiling thinly. 'You really don't have any idea just what is bothering me, do you?'

'I'm sure I don't.' She shook her head.

'That's what I thought. You're going around with your head in the clouds. I've been in love with you ever since I've known you. But you never had any time for me. Then along came Julian Kane, and the next moment you're blindly infatuated with him.'

'You're putting it a bit strong,' she commented, firming her lips.

'Not strongly enough, judging it from my position. You're making a fool of yourself, Lorna. I've already told you that, although you don't seem to think that I've got your best interests at heart. You're never going to get Kane to marry you. He's already promised to Isobel Garvin.'

Lorna caught her breath but forced herself

to remain outwardly calm. 'You seem to know a lot about it,' she responded easily.

'I've been making it my business to find out things. I don't want to see you get hurt.'

'And I don't want to hear any gossip,' she countered sharply.

He sipped his coffee, thoughtful and morose. 'We've been through this before and I came off second best,' he mused. 'So you can't see the wood for the trees! All right. You'll have to learn the hard way. It will all come out sooner or later.'

'What are you getting at?' Lorna sighed as she tried to settle her mind. She did not want a repeat of their previous altercation, but if he had learned something then she needed to know about it. She realized that he had been looking uneasy and strained for some time. 'Look, Jack, I've never encouraged you, have I? I've never said that when I recovered from my grief I'd give you the first opportunity to come calling, did I?'

'What's that got to do with it?' He

shrugged. 'I'm in love with you and that's all that matters. I've got it so bad that I'm thinking of confronting Kane to put him straight.'

'You're what?' Her face paled. 'Surely you're not serious!'

'More serious than you'll ever know.' He drained his cup and set it down, shaking his head. 'Oh, what's the use? I'm just wasting my time. But you'll come to your senses one of these fine days and I'll be standing by waiting for you. Go on and make a fool of yourself, Lorna, and afterwards I'll say that I told you so.'

He stalked out of the kitchen, leaving her to gaze after him, and, as his footsteps faded in the corridor, Lorna heaved a long, bitter sigh.

There was more to this than showed, she thought, and wondered what he had been getting at. When she pictured Julian's face she could not accept that he was planning to marry Isobel Garvin. But she could not be sure that there was nothing in what Jack had said. He was not the type to make fictitious statements.

During the rest of her duty she wondered and worried about what had been said between them, and when she left the hospital at six next morning she took the problem home with her. She went to bed, slept fitfully until two-thirty, then arose and dressed to drive out to the Manor.

It was a perfect June day, and she breathed deeply as she motored out of town. But her peace of mind had been jarred by Jack Foster's words, and she firmed her lips as she considered what he had said. He was jealous! That much was obvious, and she could not help wondering if he had said what he did in order to cause trouble between her and Julian.

She forced down her fears as she neared the Manor. Pigeons were cooing in the trees to her left as she turned into the drive. A meadowlark was a small black speck in the cloudless blue vault overhead, singing as if its very life depended upon its ceaseless song. She listened with pleasure in her heart, very much aware of the surrounding beauty, and some of the disquiet faded from her mind in the face of so much natural significance.

When she rolled to a stop in front of the house and alighted she paused to look around, and it came to her that this place was a second home. She pictured Julian's face, and a soft smile touched her lips. It wasn't until she was ringing the doorbell that she remembered she had not arranged to come to the Manor at all today.

She frowned because the fact had completely slipped her mind in the face of the concern she was feeling. What would Julian think when he saw her?

The front door was opened and Mrs Heywood peered out at her. The house-keeper seemed surprised, and her wrinkled face creased even more as she spoke.

'I was told you weren't expected today, Sister. But I'm glad you're here. Mr Julian has gone into town with his secretary and

I'm alone with Master Simon. The trouble is, I can't do anything with him.'

'Simon?' Lorna frowned. 'What's wrong?'

'He's playing up a little. There was trouble with his governess and she left early this morning. Perhaps that's what has upset the boy. He was getting along so well with this governess. Would you have a talk with him? I know you can get him to do anything.'

'Where is Simon?' Lorna asked, stepping across the threshold.

'Up in the playroom.'

'I'll go and have a chat with him.' Lorna ascended the stairs while Mrs Heywood returned to her kitchen. When she paused at the door of the playroom, Lorna heard the sound of Simon crying, and she moistened her lips as she opened the door and entered. Simon was sitting on a chair by the window, his head pillowed on his arms, his shoulders heaving as he wept. Lorna went to his side and placed a hand upon his dark head.

'What's wrong, Simon?' she demanded gently.

The boy looked up, at her, tears streaming down his face. At first he glared defiantly, until he recognised Lorna. Then he arose and hurled himself into Lorna's arms, his sobbing continuing unabated.

'This won't do,' Lorna said softly, stroking his hair. 'I don't believe I've ever seen you cry before, Simon. Tell me all about it. I'm sure we can sort it out. Crying never helped anyone solve anything.'

'I don't want you to go away and stop seeing us,' Simon said jerkily.

Lorna frowned, then suppressed a sigh. 'Who said anything about that?' she demanded.

'My governess. She was blamed for some money that went missing yesterday, and she left because she wouldn't stay in the house. Daddy was very angry, and said he was going to call the police.'

'I see.' Lorna produced a handkerchief and wiped away his tears. 'Well you've been crying over nothing, Simon, because I'm not going to stop seeing you. I think perhaps

184

you listened to what the grown-ups were saying and got it mixed up. What happened between your Daddy and your governess doesn't concern you, and I don't think you have any cause to cry. Your Daddy and I are on the best of terms, and nothing has been said about me not seeing you any more.' She paused, thinking for a moment, and Simon looked up at her. 'You know that grown-ups do say things to each other which sound very strange to children.'

He nodded, but was not entirely convinced. Lorna studied his streaked face for a moment. His eyes were swollen from crying, and she felt worried beyond comprehension, although she did not let him see her fears. What was going on beneath the surface? She had sensed an undercurrent for some time. Isobel had made her feelings rather plain after Simon had been saved from drowning. That fact alone ought to have put Lorna on her guard. But whenever she had taxed Julian about his worries he had quietly evaded the issues. She had put his manner down to difficulties in reshaping his life, but now it appeared that there could be other reasons for his periods of disquiet.

'Daddy told me yesterday that we might have to be prepared for you not wanting to see us so much in future,' said Simon, his breath catching in his throat.

'He told you that?'

'Yes. I asked him why you couldn't come to live here with us. I don't like Isobel. She is nice to me when Daddy is here, but when I'm alone with her she's nasty to me. She hates me, although she wouldn't let Daddy know that. But I can tell. I wish you were living here.'

'What exactly did your Daddy say yesterday, can you remember?' Lorna pressed.

Simon thought for a moment, then shook his head. 'I can't remember properly. He told me you had your own life to lead and we couldn't expect you to spend all your time with us.'

'I see.' Lorna concealed her feelings from

the child's worried gaze. 'Look, Simon, you needn't worry about me not seeing you again. You'll only make yourself upset and your Daddy might be angry if he learns that you've told me what he said. Why don't you lie down now and have a nap? I'll read a story to you as if it were bedtime. Would you like that?'

'Yes please. Will you read the book about the tigers?' He threw his arms around Lorna's neck and kissed her passionately.

'If we can find it.' Lorna forced away her sudden fears and smiled for the boy's benefit. She found the book and began to read to him. He held her hand tightly, but in a matter of minutes he had fallen asleep, and she eased her hand free of his grip and went down to the kitchen.

Mrs Heywood was relieved when Lorna explained the situation, but Lorna said nothing of what had upset Simon. She had a cup of tea with the housekeeper, then took her leave and drove back to town. There was a dull patch in her mind as she considered what she had learned, first from Jack Foster and now from the innocent tongue of Simon himself. She felt strangely unsettled, and wondered if she had been living in a fool's paradise ever since she had met Julian.

She considered her future but did not know what to do. She could not broach the subject to Julian because, in the past, he had not responded to her gentle probing, and she was afraid that if he was pushed he might admit that he had no intention of pursuing their association to its logical conclusion. Although she knew it would be better to learn the stark truth as soon as possible, she was only human, and the longer she could keep bad news at bay the happier she would be.

But her spirits were down to zero for the first time since she had met the Kane family, and when she reached home she put the car away and started towards the front door, but a voice called to her and she turned swiftly, half expecting to see Julian.

But it was Jack Foster, and he seemed unsteady on his feet. He came to confront her, smiling tightly, and Lorna was shocked to discover that he was tipsy. He had been drinking. She could smell the sharp tang of whisky on his breath.

'Are you off duty today?' she demanded harshly, worried that he might not be.

'Of course I am. You don't think I'd drink when there was work to be done, do you?'

'What are you doing here?' Lorna glanced around, afraid that her parents might see him and wonder at his condition. But she knew her mother and father were out at the moment.

'I want to talk to you. Why else would I be here? I don't need to see your father.' He chuckled harshly. 'I know you're off duty for the rest of the day. Let's go into the house where we'll be alone.'

'I have a better idea,' she retorted, turning to go back to the garage. 'Let's go for a drive, shall we? It might help you sober up. You'll get yourself a bad name if you're seen in this condition.'

'A drive will be better than nothing,' he said surlily, and lurched against her.

Lorna was filled with a sharp bitterness as she got the car out of the garage, for it seemed that all her happily erected dreams were about to crash down around her, leaving her with nothing but ugly reality and the problem of Jack Foster, whose love for her was exceeding his control.

NINE

'Are you sure you're off duty for the rest of today?' Lorna demanded as Foster stumbled into the front passenger seat. A searching glance at him informed her that she would have to handle him firmly but unemotionally. She was now aware that the general situation had been slipping imperceptibly for some time and she had been too happy to notice. Now the awareness filled her mind and she was a little shocked to realize that she was afraid of losing her place in the hearts of Julian and Simon.

'Duty!' He sneered, breaking into her thoughts. 'That's all my life consists of. Nothing but duty, and hoping that you'll suddenly notice me. I need to talk to you, Lorna.'

'I'll drive away from here,' she responded.

'Fasten that seat belt.'

He did so, and she drove into the country, following the road that led in the opposite direction to Cairn Manor. When she reached a lay-by she pulled in and switched off the engine.

'I'm listening now,' she said sharply. 'Let's get you settled, shall we? What's on your mind, Jack?' She asked the question although she could easily guess what was bothering him, and she accepted that she was going to have trouble convincing him that the future held nothing for them together. But she could not be angry with him because he was in love with her, for love was an emotion she could only respect.

'Don't get uppish with me,' he retorted. 'I'm not a drinking man normally and you know it. That's what is wrong. You're driving me to drink, Lorna. But you needn't feel so smugly secure yourself. The reason that set me drinking today also affects you.'

'I'm afraid I don't understand,' she said, trying to hold him off as his hard fingers grasped her upper arm. He increased the pressure when she tried to break his grip.

'You don't want to understand,' he retorted in hard, emotional tones. 'You've been wearing rose-tinted glasses for the past six weeks. You haven't seen anything of the events shaping around you. But don't forget that we know the same people.'

Lorna thought immediately of Julian and Isobel Garvin, and stiffened. Foster chuckled harshly, but she closed her mind to the sound and tried to hold back the rush of fear that threatened to overwhelm her. Simon had been badly upset by what he had been told about their future. It seemed that there was a lot going on behind the scenes.

'I thought that would pull you up short,' Foster said. 'I may be able to do you a good turn after all. I don't suppose you would turn to me if I gave you the true facts about your precious Julian Kane! But at least I can prevent you making a bigger fool of yourself than you've already done.'

'You're not making sense at all, Jack.'

Lorna glanced at her watch. The time was just after six in the evening. She had night duty at ten. 'I cannot help you in any way. I feel sorry because of the way you feel about me. I didn't realize that you were quite as serious as this and we must certainly talk it over. But not while you are in this condition. This isn't the time or the placc.'

'It's never the time or the place as far as I'm concerned, is it?' he demanded bitterly, and the agony in his voice cut through Lorna. 'Alright, take me back to town. I know I'm not going to make any impression on you. I'd better get back and sober up. I am on duty later.'

'You fool!' Lorna started the car immediately and drove back to town. She dropped Foster off at his flat, instructing him to put his head under a cold tap and to drink plenty of coffee. He stood on the pavement and watched her drive away before making any attempt to enter the tall block.

Lorna went home, and before she realized

it, time had passed and she had to prepare to go on duty. It was dark as she drove to the hospital, and she arrived with five minutes to spare. A sigh gusted from her as she tapped at the Assistant Matron's door, and Miss Hayter's voice answered immediately. Lorna composed herself as she entered the office. She went to the side of the desk where Miss Hayter sat reading through the heavy folder containing the day reports from all departments, and the older woman looked up with a welcoming smile.

'Another shift upon us, Sister,' she remarked.

'They seem to come round with monotonous regularity, don't they!' replied Lorna. 'Isn't it strange how life's routines take us completely in hand and control us?'

'They certainly do. We seem to be propelled through life and there's nothing we can do to alter the circumstances. But I must say that you've had a change of attitude towards life since we last had a chat. Wasn't it about two months ago? How are you making out now? Shaking off your grief, aren't you?'

'Yes.' Lorna nodded. 'It went suddenly and I'm practically back to normal. Reflecting upon it, I must say that it all seems like a rather bad dream now.'

'It's surprising how that sort of thing suddenly lifts. Of course it doesn't leave your mind completely, but if you can go on living without too much pain then the whole thing falls into perspective. Have you found a new interest? That's what usually brings about a change of attitude.'

Lorna thought of Julian and Simon and nodded slowly.

'Yes,' she agreed. 'I have new interests.'

'I'm glad for your sake! It was dreadful to see you going about your duties with such a burden on your mind. Would I be showing too much interest and curiosity if I asked whether Jack Foster has anything to do with your sudden uplift?'

'I'm afraid you're rather a long way out. Jack does care a great deal about me and he's never made a secret of it. But I'm afraid he could never be more than a friend.'

'I think I'd better change the subject,' Miss Hayter retorted with a smile. 'But I'm happy that you have climbed out of that rut. It is a rut. I know from personal experience. But to get back to duty. Here are the day reports and I'll leave you to get on with it. You don't need me wasting your time with idle chatter. A night sister's lot is a very busy one.'

'That's true.' Lorna smiled as she sat down in the seat which Miss Hayter vacated, and when her superior had departed she began to check through the day reports, making a list of all the patients who might need special nursing during the night. She double-checked the Seriously Ill list, then concentrated upon all new admissions and post-operatives. It helped considerably to make a few notes on those patients who might need her most, and a few moments spent now in fruitful writing could prevent an emergency later in the night.

When she was satisfied that all relevant details were either in her notebook or her mind, Lorna prepared to make her first complete round of the wards. She called Switchboard to leave with the operator an itinerary of her movements, for the telephone was a vital link with the administration of the hospital, and it was important that members of the staff could be contacted swiftly.

Lorna found herself hoping that she would not come across Jack Foster during her tour of duty, and that he would not have to be called out. She tried to keep her personal thoughts out of the forefront of her mind because she had so many facts and snippets of information about the patients to remember that she could not afford to let her thoughts wander. She kept an eye on the time as she progressed, for she did not want to fall behind her self-imposed schedule. If she did get behind and an emergency arose it could result in confusion.

She went into Male Medical, checking her

notebook and her mind for details of the patients here likely to be needing her attention. She saw the night nurse and learned of the first complication.

'Sister, Switchboard just called for you. The R.S.O. is with a patient in Male Surgical, and he thinks he'll have to operate before morning.'

'Thank you, Nurse. I'll be in Male Surgical myself very shortly so I'll see the R.S.O. then.'

She went on, not wanting to see Jack Foster. She entered Male Surgical and found the R.S.O. at the bedside of the patient who would need the operation, and they discussed the case for some moments. As Night Sister, Lorna would be expected to assist if the case were complicated. There was a Staff Nurse on duty, with a Theatre Sister on call if required, but it was the practice for Night Sister to take the case if she were not too busy. The Staff Nurse handled all the simple cases, but Lorna always welcomed the opportunity to participate because it enabled her to keep up to date with Theatre practice.

After promising to scrub for the case if required, Lorna went on. She checked with the night nurses in the wards, getting the usual complaints about chores that had not been completed by the nurses on the previous shifts, about missing laundry and misplaced keys, and a hundred other matters that threatened to keep her occupied half the night on frivolous things.

Switchboard called her half a dozen times, leaving messages for her with the various night nurses, informing her of unexpected emergencies and problems, and Lorna jotted down items she might need for future reference. But it was almost midnight by the time she returned to the office. When she sat down to bring her reports up to date she tried to relax for a moment, but her mind immediately became filled with thoughts of Julian and Simon, and she sighed as she forced herself to concentrate upon duty.

She now had a very good idea of the night

situation in the hospital and quickly brought her paperwork up to date. She was almost finished when footsteps sounded in the corridor outside, and her heart seemed to miss a beat as she feared it might be Foster. She wondered what would happen if he had to assist with the emergency operation, for he had been drinking rather heavily. She knew a great deal of disquiet as she listened to the footsteps and judged them to be female.

The next moment the door was opened and her assistant, Staff Nurse Hall, appeared.

'I was called to Children's,' Nurse Hall explained. 'It's all right now. Shall I start the jabs list?'

'Yes, please carry on. There's likely to be an emergency op that I'll have to scrub for, so you'll have to take over while I'm in Theatre. Try and keep to schedule, just in case. I'll check with you later.'

'Fine.' Staff Nurse Hall was in her middle-twenties, a tall, slender brunette. She smiled as she met Lorna's gaze. 'By the way, I ran into Mr Foster earlier and he said he wanted to talk to you as soon as possible. I told him I'd pass on the message.'

'I'm trying to avoid him,' Lorna confessed.

'I had noticed he's been getting rather ardent. He didn't seem to be in top form when I saw him. I thought he looked ill. If I didn't know him better I'd suspect that he'd been drinking before he came on duty.'

'He's got a lot on his mind,' Lorna said, and wondered why she was making excuses for him.

'I don't wonder at it. He's supposed to be in love with you, but I've seen him several times lately in the company of Isobel Garvin, and she's trouble for any man.'

'Isobel Garvin! She's Julian Kane's secretary.'

'That's right. There's only one Isobel Garvin, thank Heaven. In a town this size, everyone knows everything that goes on. But you know her, Sister. You know the

Kanes! I was forgetting. I'm sorry.'

'You've got nothing to be sorry for,' retorted Lorna. 'Jack Foster is at liberty to go around with whom he likes. But it is strange that he took up with Isobel. I would have thought they were poles apart in everything. But I suppose they met when she visited Julian here after his accident.'

'All I can say is that if he prefers her to you then he needs to have his head examined. But I heard a rumour that Isobel had set her cap at Julian Kane, and she usually gets what she goes after. Oh well. Everyone to his or her fancy. I'll take the jabs list and get back to work. There's a pot of tea in the kitchen. It's fresh, if you fancy one. I made it just before I went down to Children's.'

'Thanks, but I'm too busy to stop just now.' Lorna suppressed a sigh as Nurse Hall took a list from the desk and departed. For some moments she sat thinking over what had been said, and wondered about Jack Foster's attitude. He kept professing un-dying love for her and yet he was seeing

Isobel. But if Isobel was intent upon winning over Julian then why was she bothering with Foster? They were so patently incompatible that there had to be less obvious reasons why they were seeing each other.

Lorna firmed her lips. It seemed to be such a complicated situation. She shook her head, then realized that she was wasting time on personal thoughts and brought her mind back to duty. Yet she could not prevent stray thoughts creeping up from time to time. She was in love with Julian and thought the world of Simon. They had replaced her own lost family, but it seemed that there was a great danger of losing them also, and she would suffer greatly if they had to vacate their places now. But she was mainly concerned about Simon. He had been so terribly upset the day before. Another governess had departed from his life, and Julian had told the boy not to expect Lorna to remain too long in their lives. What had happened behind the scenes that she did not know about?

There was a knock at the door and Lorna jerked free of her thoughts and looked up as Jack Foster entered the office. His face was set in harsh lines and he jerked forward a chair to sit down heavily. Lorna gazed intently at him, wondering if he had continued drinking after she had dropped him off outside his flat.

'I've been trying to catch up with you half the night,' he said sourly. 'You're like a butterfly, Lorna. You never settle long in one place. Where were you thirty minutes ago?'

'I know where I'll be in another thirty minutes,' she retorted. 'In Theatre, assisting with the emergency op. You'll also be in on that, Jack, and you'd better make some attempt at appearing normal. You drank some more after I dropped you off earlier, didn't you?'

'I couldn't care less about the operation or anything else,' he said harshly. 'I can't take much more of this. You're driving me crazy, Lorna.'

'I can smell whisky on your breath from here,' she accused. 'You can't go into Theatre like that. You'll be discovered, and it would probably cost you your job. If you were dismissed for being intoxicated on duty your whole career would be ruined. You'd never get a job in another hospital as long as you lived.'

'I've got to make you see sense,' he said, not listening to her words. 'You'll be wasting your life if you try to marry Kane.'

'You seem to know a great deal about my personal life,' she observed in a thin tone.

'So it is true! You are planning to hook Kane.'

'You say you're madly in love with me, Jack. Is that true?'

'Of course it is. You must be blind if you can't see that.'

'Then why have you been seeing so much of Isobel Garvin if you can't live without me?'

He stared at her for several moments, his face grimly set, his eyes unblinking. He had stiffened at her words, but now his shoulders slumped. 'Who told you I'd been seeing her?' he demanded. 'Have you had someone watching me?'

'Why would I want to do that? I have no interest in you and there is nothing between us. But I can put two and two together, Jack, and it's fairly simple to work out that Isobel is after Julian and has somehow enlisted your aid to keep me away from him.'

'You're quite the detective, aren't you? Listen, anything I've done is to protect your future. I know Isobel well enough to realize that when she sets her cap at a man she usually gets him. She wants Julian Kane, and a good, honest girl like you doesn't stand a chance. You've had a lot of heart-ache in your life, Lorna, and I'm trying to spare you more.'

'You have no right to interfere in my life, Jack, and this is the last time I shall tell you. At the moment I regard you as a friend, and I could never look upon you as a potential husband. So the sooner you accept that fact the better for all concerned.' She held his startled gaze. 'Have I made myself clear?'

His facial muscles worked spasmodically for a moment, his eyes showing his emotion. Then he shook his head slowly, as if denying to himself what she had said.

'I'll never be able to stop loving you, Lorna. It's just one of those things.' He paused, his expression hardening. 'All right. I don't expect you to fall in love with me just like that.' He snapped his fingers. 'I know what you've been suffering and you deserve a break. That's why I want to stop you making a fool of yourself over Julian Kane. He's no good for you. I can see it if you can't.'

'Don't you see that it's the child I'm really concerned about?' she demanded, losing her patience. 'Poor Simon! He hasn't had much of a life since his mother died. I only want to bring him a little joy, and that's what I've succeeded in doing since I've been seeing them. I'm not selfishly motivated like Isobel Garvin. All she sees is a rich husband, and it doesn't matter to her that Simon is lonely and unhappy. You're selfish too, Jack. You're thinking only of yourself in this. Now I'm telling you that I want to hear no more about your feelings for me or what you're planning for my benefit. I'm old enough to make my own decisions, and that is the way it will be.'

She was thoroughly aroused by the time she stopped talking, and stared into his stiff face. He watched her for a moment while the silence grew heavy, and was aware that anything he said now could only worsen his position. The telephone shrilled loudly, startling Lorna, and she moistened her lips as she snatched up the receiver.

'Night Sister.' Her voice trembled as she spoke.

'This is Switchboard, Sister. Have you seen Mr Foster? He's wanted for the emergency. Would you also scrub for it?'

'Yes. Thank you. Mr Foster is here with me and I'll give him the message. We'll go straight along to the Theatre.'

Foster got to his feet as she hung up, and staggered a little as he turned to the door. He said nothing and departed, and Lorna frowned as she watched him. Then she drew a shuddering breath, hoping that she had cleared the air between them. But she intended to have a chat with Isobel Garvin as soon as the opportunity presented itself.

But duty was pressing and she left the office to go to Theatre. She eased her mind of personal thoughts and climbed the stairs instead of using the lift. When she reached the corridor outside the Theatre she paused to listen to the familiar sounds that came to her ears. But there was no time for musing and she entered quickly. She found Staff Nurse Thompson carrying out the last-minute preparations, and discovered that, as usual, Nurse Thompson had been efficient and competent. Lorna praised the girl and was rewarded with a smile. She carried out the usual checks, and by the time they had finished the rest of the surgical team had arrived.

Foster's eyes looked sullenly over the top of his mask, and he hardly spoke to Mr James, the R.S.O. He glanced at Lorna briefly but looked away, and she was relieved when the patient arrived. She had checked Foster critically upon his appearance, but he did not seem to be any the worse for drink, although his hands were trembling slightly. Lorna was relieved that he was only assisting. If he had been scheduled to handle the operation himself she would have voiced strong objections.

They were professional enough to forget personal differences when on duty and the operation proceeded. At first Lorna was stiff with apprehension, for she was certain that Foster was not completely capable and efficient, and was afraid that he would make an elementary mistake which would immediately be spotted by Mr James. But nothing significant developed and within the hour the patient was being returned to the ward.

Lorna felt limp with nervous reaction and

her eyes were dull as she watched Foster's departure behind the R.S.O. When he had removed his mask, Foster's face looked drawn and pale, his eyes glassy. But he hurried away and Lorna pulled down her mask and peeled off her gloves.

'I'm sorry, but I'll have to leave you to do the cleaning up,' she told Staff Nurse Thompson. 'I must get back to my duties.'

'Thank you, Sister. Would you like a cup of coffee before you go? There'll be one in Theatre Sister's office.'

'I'd like one but I really don't have the time.' Lorna smiled. 'Let me know if there's anything else I can do.'

She departed quickly, fighting off her tiredness as she went back to her office to check with her assistant. Once again her personal thoughts came pushing back to the forefront of her mind, easily overpowering her weary determination. She frowned as she mentally struggled for superiority. But she decided that she would do something about the situation when she went off duty.

It was a time for confrontation. She had put Jack Foster in his place. Now she would go a step further. No matter the outcome, she would consider Simon's interests and put the boy's welfare and happiness first, and she would force the issues in no uncertain manner.

Having reached the decision, Lorna was faintly surprised that some of her fears immediately dissipated. She found the remaining hours of night duty passing more easily, and at six in the morning she handed over her responsibilities to her relief and left the hospital.

First she would have six hours sleep. Afterwards she would go through with her determination to clarify the situation. But as she went homeward she experienced fresh doubts and fears, and had to fight off the impulse to change her mind. It was likely that her actions would rupture the fine understanding that had grown up between her and Julian. It could ruin her future happiness. But she realized that she was adult enough to face any emotional upheaval. Simon was not and had to be protected. That knowledge alone made her face up to the harsh facts.

TEN

Lorna counted herself fortunate that her parents were not up when she reached home, and she quickly had a light meal before going to bed. She was so tired that despite her teeming thoughts she closed her eyes and drifted immediately into an uneasy sleep. She knew nothing more until she awoke later to find the bedroom stifling. The sun was shining upon the drawn curtains and the interior was like a bakery. She arose and pulled on her dressing gown, then went to the window and drew the curtains, blinking in the strong afternoon glare. She glanced at her watch. The time was almost 2.30.

A sigh escaped her as she prepared to go out, and a cooling shower refreshed her and chased the last of her tiredness out of her system. She put on a lightweight green dress then went down for her meal. For some unknown reason she was nervous about confronting her mother.

Mrs Parry was sunning herself on the terrace but took off her sunglasses and got to her feet when Lorna appeared at her side.

'Hello, dear,' she greeted cheerfully. 'Wasn't it too hot to sleep?'

'I was too tired to be concerned about the weather,' Lorna responded.

'From what I can remember of my nursing career, night duty was always like that. Have you eaten yet or have you just come down?'

'I'm going to eat now. Will you be using the car this afternoon? I want to go out to the Manor.'

'No, I don't want it. But I'd like to talk to you on a personal level, Lorna. I don't want you to think that I'm prying, or anything like that, but I am your mother and I do have your best interests at heart.'

'That sounds rather ominous.' Lorna smiled as she met her mother's gaze.

'What's on your mind? If you can't talk to me heart to heart then nobody can.'

'I've heard some rumours about Jack Foster. Have you two been quarrelling? Is anything wrong?'

'No. There's nothing wrong. Jack is in love with me. That much I do know. But I can't reciprocate his feelings and he's finding that hard to accept.'

'Poor Jack! But it's Julian Kane for you, isn't it?'

'You're very perceptive!' Lorna smiled. 'But don't let us be premature about this. I have the feeling that nothing will come from my association with Julian. In fact that has almost come to an end now.'

'Is that what has upset you?'

'I'm not upset.' Lorna spoke firmly.

'Have you had a difference of opinion with Julian?' Mrs Parry persisted. 'What has brought about this change of attitudes?'

'Outwardly there have been no changes, and that's really the disturbing factor. But perhaps I've been reading too much into the situation. From the start I really only concerned myself with Simon's welfare, and as far as that goes I've succeeded in what I set out to do. He's a very much happier boy now.'

'But his happiness is built up on his regard for you. The moment you walk out of his life his world will collapse like a house built of cards. Don't you see that he can never be happy unless he has both you and his father? I saw this problem arising from the outset. The only way to overcome it would be for you to overlook your personal feelings and ensure that what you do for the child is not coloured or governed by your emotions for his father.'

'I have been thinking along those lines, Mother. I'm afraid that I did allow myself to be attracted to Julian, and lately my desire to see him has outweighed the facts of the situation and poor Simon's needs have been pushed into the background. But everything was proceeding nicely until outside factors began to interfere.'

'In the shape of Isobel Garvin, I should think,' Mrs Parry said quietly. She nodded. 'I think that you'll find a certain situation existed at Cairn Manor before you walked in, Lorna. It didn't evolve after your advent. I expect it changed because of your appearance. Isobel Garvin is a scheming woman, so I've been led to believe. She's determined to marry Julian Kane, and because you've appeared on the scene she is compelled to do something about you. Is this what is upsetting you? Has her influence caused any straining of the relationship that's grown up between you and Julian?'

'Not directly.' Lorna shook her head. 'I think she's being more deceitful than that. Instead of openly trying to cause trouble, probably because she's afraid of letting Julian discover her real character, she's using more devious means.' She went on to explain about Isobel's association with Jack Foster. 'I think they are working together to cause a rift in my friendship with Julian in the hope that Julian will marry Isobel and I'll turn to Jack.'

'So that's it.' Mrs Parry shook her head slowly as she thought about it. 'No wonder you're upset, Lorna.'

'I'm not upset for myself, Mother. I'm only concerned about Simon. But I'm going to the Manor now to force the issues a little. I've decided that my life can take any shock that comes along, but Simon needs consideration and gentle handling. I'm going to put his needs before my own inclinations and let Julian see just what is going on around him. It may alienate his feelings towards me but I don't care.'

'I think that course of action can only clear the air,' said Mrs Parry. 'But you could be playing into Isobel's hands. She is far too clever to cause trouble herself. She obviously wants you to show yourself in a bad light.'

'Well she won't be disappointed.' Lorna smiled. 'I'm going to do something positive.'

'I hope you won't be too upset afterwards,'

her mother retorted.

'This uncertainty is more than I can bear, Mother. It will be something to get a settlement one way or another.'

'I'll keep my fingers crossed for you,' Mrs Parry said softly.

Lorna found her appetite almost non-existent when she sat down to her meal, but she was filled with determination and ate methodically, her thoughts occupied with what she intended doing. Afterwards she went out to the garage and took the car, and there was a blend of relief and tension inside her as she drove off to Cairn Manor.

She did not see her surroundings despite the fact that the sun was shining and it was a glorious day. As she drew nearer to the Manor she found her speed slowing. But she went on, turning into the drive and approaching the house. When she switched off she sat for a moment listening to the birds singing while she tried to enjoy the peacefulness and beauty of her surroundings. For a moment it seemed that the tensions and worries of the past twenty-four hours had been the product of a bad dream. But reality was never far away, she knew, and alighted from the car and walked up the steps to the big front door.

Mrs Heywood came in answer to her knock, and the housekeeper frowned for a moment, making Lorna's sensitive mind believe that she was not welcome.

'Mr Julian isn't at home. He had to go out on urgent business. You arranged to come out this afternoon, did you?'

'Yes.' Lorna did not let her disappointment show. 'Business before pleasure, of course. Did he leave a message for me?'

'I'm afraid he didn't say anything. He was in such a hurry when he went out. But you don't have to go. Simon has been asking about you all day.'

'How is he after yesterday?'

'He had a troubled night and a bit of a temperature this morning. I was tempted to call in the doctor but the lad seemed brighter after breakfast. Children are like that! Up one moment, down the next. He has his share of troubles though. I feel so sorry for him. I thought his troubles would be over when you came into his life, but it isn't so.' Mrs Heywood shook her head. 'But what am I thinking of, keeping you standing on the doorstep? Whenever you enter this house it's like letting in the sunshine. Come into the kitchen and I'll make a pot of tea.'

Lorna warmed to the old lady and followed her into the house, fighting down her disappointment. They entered the kitchen and Lorna sat down. She watched Mrs Heywood making tea, and there were a hundred questions she wanted to ask but dare not. It would not be right to question the housekeeper about matters concerning the master of the house.

'Where is Simon?' she asked. 'Has he finished his lessons for the day?'

'He hasn't had many of those lately,' replied Mrs Heywood. 'I don't know how all this will come out. As I said, I thought your coming on the scene would change matters, and it appeared to do so at first. But deep-laid plans are difficult to uproot.'

Lorna did not question that statement, and she was thoughtful as they drank tea. Mrs Heywood seemed to be in a resentful mood but Lorna realized that she was not the cause of it.

'Where is Simon?' she repeated when she had finished her tea.

'In the stables, I shouldn't wonder. Now his governess has been chased away he's left in Miss Garvin's hands, and she went after him some time ago.'

Lorna glanced at her watch and suppressed a sigh. 'Perhaps I'd better go home again, Mrs Heywood, and if Mr Julian returns he can telephone me.'

'Don't go,' the housekeeper replied quickly. 'If Simon found that you'd come and gone without seeing him he'd be even more upset. He knows you're supposed to be coming. He's talked of nothing else all morning.'

'All right.' Lorna nodded. 'I'll go and look

for him. He went to see his pony, did you say?'

'That's what he told me. I expect he's somewhere around.'

Lorna left the house by the kitchen door and made her way around the outhouses to the rear. When she came to the stables there was no sign of Simon and the pony was not in its stall. She went through the stables and opened the top half of the rear door, peering out across the wide paddock, and there was a harsh expression upon her face, a product of her thoughts, but it softened when she saw Simon astride his pony, trotting across the short grass.

A shrill voice echoed through the stillness and Lorna frowned as she looked around. To the far right, at the end of the paddock, Isobel Garvin was standing with her hands on her hips, and even at that distance Lorna could detect fury in the woman's tone.

'Simon, this is the last time I shall call you! Now come to me. I shall be forced to punish you for disobedience if you don't. Now come here at once.'

Lorna firmed her lips as she watched, and her first impulse was to go out and discover what was wrong. But she stifled her reaction because she did not want to interfere or usurp Isobel's authority. With Simon's governess gone, the secretary was taking charge of the boy. But it was obvious that Isobel was fast losing her temper.

Simon turned the pony and went back towards the gesticulating secretary. Isobel subsided as the child drew nearer, and began to walk towards Simon. But as the distance between them lessened, Simon slowed his pace, and Lorna felt a tightening of her nerves as she watched. At the last moment, Simon swerved the pony to the left and sent it at a canter in the opposite direction once more. Isobel shouted angrily and broke into a run, and it seemed that she might catch the child. But Simon kicked with his heels and the pony increased its gait. Isobel halted, calling furiously in a strident voice.

Lorna shook her head and began to open the lower half of the door, but she paused once more when she saw Simon swinging around again and trotting back towards the secretary. The previous manoeuvre was repeated, Simon turning away at the last moment. But on this occasion his timing was inaccurate and Isobel ran forward as the child urged the pony away. Simon cried out in sudden fear as Isobel appeared at his side, grasping the reins and halting the pony.

'You're a naughty boy and I shall punish you severely for this,' shouted Isobel. 'Ever since Sister Parry came into your life I've been unable to do anything with you.' She held the bridle and shook the animal's head violently. The pony became frightened and tried to back away. But Isobel controlled it and her penetrating voice went on and on.

Lorna could see that Simon was badly frightened. The boy was clinging to the pony's mane, his sharp cries echoing across the paddock. Isobel shook the pony's head once more, and this time the animal reared, then kicked backwards, almost unseating Simon. Lorna caught her breath, opening the stable door instinctively to go hurrying across the paddock.

'You've had too much of your own way and been allowed too many distractions,' Isobel was shouting. 'Your father has no idea how to bring up a child, and the advice he's received from Sister Parry has only made matters worse.' She slapped the pony across the nose and the animal bucked and kicked furiously, almost unseating Simon, who cried out in fear. 'For a start I'll make you so scared of this animal that you won't ever want to ride it again. I'm going to change the situation back to what it was before your precious Sister Parry came on the scene.'

Lorna could see that Isobel was losing her control, that she was permitting her anger to push her too far. The pony was being frightened into fractiousness, and Lorna was horrified that Simon could be subjected to such callous treatment. She realized that the secretary was using Simon as an excuse to bring her feelings towards the general situation into play and was venting her spite on the child because he had been instrumental in bringing Lorna into their lives. Lorna began to run forward, filled with consternation at this display of ill-humour, and now she could understand why Simon had been upset during the past few days if this was a sample of Isobel's treatment of him.

Isobel forced up the pony's head and the animal tried to break away from her. Simon cried out as he felt himself slipping from the saddle, and it seemed to Lorna that Isobel was intent upon forcing the child to lose his seat.

'Isobel!' Lorna called loudly and angrily. 'Stop that.'

'Lorna!' There was a world of relief in Simon's voice, and his pale face turned in her direction.

Isobel swung around, startled by Lorna's intervention, and Lorna wished that Julian had been with her. Isobel's anger had made her forget her surroundings. She changed expression at sight of Lorna and released her hold upon the pony's bridle. The animal snorted and whirled, and the next moment it was racing away across the paddock in blind flight, with Simon clinging to the saddle, yelling in extreme fear as he was bumped and jolted.

Lorna ran forward but was unable to intercept the pony. She passed Isobel, who seemed rooted to the spot. Lorna glanced at the woman's set face, and was appalled by the spiteful expression she saw. But her concern was for Simon and she ran swiftly in pursuit, although she realized that she could not catch the fleeing animal.

By some miracle Simon was not thrown to the ground. He clung with all his childish strength to the pony's mane, and held on until the animal reached the end of the paddock. There the pony halted and stood trembling, and Simon slid from the saddle and ran several tottering paces from it before crumpling to the grass in a storm of hysterical weeping.

Lorna hurried to the boy and dropped to her knees, taking him into her arms. She comforted him, talking softly to reassure him, and Simon cried unrestrainedly.

'You're not hurt!' Lorna soothed. 'Don't cry any more. There's nothing to be afraid of now. Let's go and look at your pony. He's frightened too. He needs you to tell him there's nothing wrong.'

'I don't want the pony any more,' Simon cried. 'I'm frightened of it now.'

Lorna got to her feet and led Simon back to the pony, which was highly nervous and backed away cautiously.

'Look how afraid he is,' said Lorna. 'You're the only friend he's got. Let's calm him, then tell him there's nothing to fear.' She left Simon and walked to the pony, which backed away, tossing its head and rolling its eyes. 'There now,' she said soothingly. 'There's nothing to be afraid of.' She reached out slowly and patted the animal's neck, then took hold of the reins. The pony shied a little but Lorna held it firmly, and Simon came hesitantly to her side and patted the animal.

Lorna sighed in relief and looked around. Isobel was standing motionless on the spot she had occupied when Lorna made her presence known. For a moment they stared at one another, then Isobel turned abruptly to depart. She walked away stiffly, still very angry.

'Just a moment, Isobel,' Lorna called, and tightened her grip upon the reins as the pony pulled nervously, still upset and wary. 'I want to talk to you.'

'I don't like Isobel,' Simon quavered. 'She hates me. Ever since I told her I like you better she's been hurting me. I told Daddy I wanted you to come and live with us but he said I had to get used to living without you.'

'When did he tell you this?' Lorna demanded.

'This morning.' Simon looked up at Lorna with troubled gaze. 'He said it had been a mistake to let you get into our lives because I would be hurt when you didn't come any more.'

Lorna sighed as she wondered where Julian had gone. Was he deliberately avoiding her? It seemed that he was having second thoughts about the situation and regretted its commencement. Isobel had probably worked her wiles upon him to such an extent that he was unable to look beyond her now. He had professed love for Lorna, but obviously he'd had trouble trying to make that particular dream come true, and when he reached the crossroads of decision he had decided that his feelings for Isobel were more powerful than his regard for Simon's future.

'You said you would never stop coming to see me,' Simon said tremulously, his thin tone jerking Lorna from her thoughts.

'I wouldn't want to, Simon, but it is possible that certain people wouldn't be happy with my comings and goings.'

'That's what Daddy said.' Simon sniffed

miserably. 'Why should it hurt other people if you kept coming to see me?'

'When people grow up they acquire emotions you wouldn't understand right now. Some people would find a stranger like me something of a nuisance coming to see you.' Lorna smiled coldly. She could picture Isobel's face, and knew the woman had no consideration for Simon. The child would have a miserable life when Isobel became his stepmother.

'I wish I didn't have to live here any longer,' said Simon. 'I want to live with you, Lorna.'

'I'm afraid that's impossible. Your father will make a good life for you, Simon. I'm sure you'll soon forget me. But we'll probably see each other now and again. But don't worry about it now. Ride the pony around for a bit. I'm going to talk to Isobel and I don't want you to overhear what I have to say. I'll come back to you shortly.'

'The pony will run away with me again,' said Simon fearfully.

'No he won't. He's calm again now. Isobel upset him. But he knows you're always kind to him. Just take him quietly. I'll watch you for a few moments. Off you go!'

Simon was nervous, but Lorna knew the boy had to ride the pony again immediately or he might completely lose his nerve. Simon patted the pony, then permitted Lorna to help him into the saddle. The next moment the boy trotted away as if nothing had happened and Lorna sighed in relief. When she turned to look for Isobel she discovered that the woman had gone from the paddock.

Lorna wouldn't leave Simon alone on the pony for fear of more trouble, so she waited patiently until the boy had recovered his poise. When Simon came trotting back to where Lorna stood he was cheerful once more.

'It's all right,' he said chirpily. 'I'm not frightened any more. I'll take the pony into his stall and give him some water and oats. But I don't want Isobel taking me out on riding exercise again. Please will you tell Daddy, Lorna?'

'I'll certainly tell him. We can't have a repetition of what I saw earlier.'

They went to the stable and Lorna watched the child grooming the pony. When Simon was engrossed in what he was doing, Lorna left him.

'I'm going into the house to talk to Isobel, Simon,' she said. 'I want you to come in when you've finished here. I'll be waiting for you.'

'I'll come, I promise. Don't worry about me, Lorna. I'm all right now.'

Lorna smiled wryly as she left the stable. Poor Simon! The boy knew no happiness, and the small pleasures he had gained since Lorna came into his life looked like evaporating. A shadow touched Lorna's mind and she compressed her lips. It seemed that her only pleasure – having Simon's and Julian's company – was coming to an end. Isobel would see to that. Simon had said as much. He had evidently overheard a conversation between his father and Isobel and their future had been settled. But Lorna was concerned for Simon's sake. She was certain that Isobel was not a fit person to have charge of the boy. She had none of Simon's interests at heart.

Yet there was nothing Lorna could do and the knowledge was bitter. When she saw Julian again she would talk very seriously to him, but she guessed that he would merely tell her it was all over between them. She dreaded the confrontation but it had to come, and she was sensible enough to realize that the sooner it was arranged the better for all concerned. But Isobel was another matter, and Lorna entered the house like an angry she-bear with cubs to defend.

Pausing in the hall, Lorna looked around, and Isobel's cold tones came to her from the doorway of the drawing room. Lorna saw the woman standing there and a coldness descended upon her as she went towards Isobel.

'Come in,' Isobel said. 'I suppose you'll want to have your money's worth before you go. I think we ought to have had a serious chat when you first came on the scene.'

She backed into the drawing room and Lorna followed, closing the heavy door. They faced each other across the width of the room, and a tight anger settled upon Lorna when she saw the mocking smile on Isobel's sneering lips. She crossed the room until there was barely an arm's length between them, and there was the glint of battle in her eyes.

'You could remain silent and save us both a lot of hard feelings,' snapped Isobel, getting in first blow. 'You forced your way into this situation, pretending affection for Simon just to get into Julian's good books.'

'You shouldn't judge everyone by your own standards,' Lorna countered. 'Let us leave Julian out of this for a moment. My only concern is for Simon, and the scene I witnessed in the paddock makes me afraid for the child's future. You have no interest in him, and the only reason you force yourself to have anything to do with him is because he brings you closer to Julian.'

'My designs are clear, at least. I don't conceal my hopes behind a screen of deceit. You have no more regard for Simon's future than I. You've used the boy from the start, and I've made Julian aware of that fact.'

'You even enlisted Jack Foster's aid to get at me.' Lorna fought to control her anger. 'I didn't think anyone could sink so low.'

'All is fair in love and war. You never had a chance from the start. You didn't know that. But now that you have lost your chance you could at least bow out gracefully. You've made Simon worse than he was. He's attracted to you and has turned against me, which will make life that much harder for him. I was training him nicely before you appeared on the scene. Now I shall have to start all over again. If you have any thought for the boy at all then you'll leave the estate now and never come back.'

There was so much Lorna wanted to say,

but suddenly she could see the hopelessness of her position and realized that she would only make matters worse by trying to force the issues over Simon. If she left now and never returned, Simon would get over his disappointment in a few days and settle down to his new way of life. Julian would see to it that the child was not unhappy, for he was now aware of the boy's presence. And perhaps Isobel would mend her ways when she finally got what she was after.

'I'm merely wasting my breath on you,' she said quietly. 'You're as impervious as stone. I didn't know what the situation was when I first came here, but if I had my attitude would have been different. I had no interest in Julian in the first place and I assure you that I am not the kind of person to push myself between another woman and her plans. My only concern is for Simon, and I can see that my continued presence is causing him more distress, although he would be far happier having me around instead of you. But I'll leave now and I won't come back. I'll talk to Simon and explain as gently as possible that I have to go. Just try to be patient with him, Isobel. All he really needs is love and understanding.'

'Just walk out now,' retorted Isobel, her eyes gleaming in triumph. 'The least said, soonest mended. I'll handle Simon, and with you out of the way he'll settle down all right. Forget about him. Go back to your own kind and leave us alone. Jack Foster is in love with you, and he's going to pieces because you snub him. Give him a break, if you want to help someone.'

'I'll say goodbye to Simon,' Lorna retorted firmly. There was a chill sensation in her breast, as if her heart had frozen solid.

'And what about Julian? Are you going to embarrass him with a mushy goodbye?'

'You can tell him that I've taken my leave of Simon and that I won't bother him again.' Lorna turned to the door, and Isobel chuckled harshly as she departed.

Simon was still busy in the stable when

Lorna returned there, and she heard the boy singing to himself as he groomed the pony. Lorna paused and watched for a moment, and somewhere deep inside a painful spasm hurt her with sudden intensity. But Lorna knew she had to remain unemotional, if only for Simon's sake, and she forced a smile as the child, sensing her presence, suddenly looked around.

'You look as if you're doing a good job, Simon,' Lorna remarked in cheery tones.

'You don't look very pleased,' the boy replied perceptively. 'Did Isobel say nasty things to you?'

'I've had a very serious talk with Isobel, and I think she'll treat you a lot better in future. But all this trouble could have been avoided, Simon, if you had tried to do what Isobel asked.'

'She hates me.' There was intense emotion in the young voice.

'That's not true. She was upset when you turned to me and showed your feelings all too plainly. When you get older, Simon, you will learn to conceal your emotions like everyone else does. Just look at me now. Would you be able to tell just by looking at me that I'm very sad right now?'

Simon subjected her to a critical gaze, then shook his head emphatically. 'No,' he decided. 'Your eyes look a bit brighter, that's all. But what are you sad about, Lorna?'

'I came here this afternoon to tell you, but the trouble I found when I arrived pushed it into the background. Now I have to tell you.' Lorna suppressed a sigh and tried to hold down her feelings. But this promised to be the hardest moment of her life. She had to go through with it for Simon's sake, and it was the only fact which gave her resolution.

ELEVEN

'There is something wrong,' said Simon in sudden alarm. 'What has happened, Lorna?'

'Nothing is wrong. I have some good news, as a matter of fact. I'm being promoted.'

'What does that mean?'

'I'm being given a better job with more responsibility and more pay.' It was a white lie, but Lorna felt justified in using it.

'That is good news, but you said you're sad.' There was keen speculation in Simon's eyes.

'I'm sad because this promotion will mean I must leave here to go to another hospital, and I shan't be able to see you for a long time, Simon.'

'Oh no!' The cry was wrung from the child's heart, and he came running to

Lorna, who opened her arms and gathered him to her breast. 'You can't go away, Lorna. I'll be left all alone!'

Lorna buried her face against the boy's shoulder and blinked rapidly to get rid of the shimmering tears that threatened to blind her. She dared not show her emotions. She had to appear light-hearted and casual in order to lessen Simon's sorrow.

'You won't be all alone,' she whispered. 'You still have your father. Anyway, I thought we were good friends. If you are my friend then you'll be happy about my good news. I would be if I were in your place.'

'I am glad for you. But I'll miss you while you're away.' Simon's voice was muffled.

'That's how it should be,' Lorna said lightly. 'It proves you do care for me. I'll miss you too. But we have to live our lives, Simon, and sometimes we have to do things we don't like that cause us pain. But always remember that we are friends, and I will see you again.'

'When will you go?' asked Simon tremulously, and when he looked into Lorna's face there were fresh tears in his eyes.

'I have to leave now. You must go into the house and see Isobel. Tell her that you're sorry for not being nice to her and she will accept your apology and treat you all the better. Try to look upon her as a friend and she will act like one. I'm sure you will be a lot happier in future, Simon.'

'But will I see you again?'

'Of course you will.' Lorna smiled, although her heart felt as if it were breaking. 'Come to my car with me and see me off. Just think of all the sick people who need me. You're a lot happier than they are, and more fortunate. But you will come to understand that as you get older.'

Simon nodded uncertainly and stifled a sob. They left the stable and walked hand in hand to where Lorna's car was parked. Lorna bent and kissed the boy, then smiled, but the anguish showing on Simon's face was almost more than she could bear.

'Run along now to Isobel,' Lorna said

quietly. 'I have to be on my way. I'll telephone you often, if I may, just to talk to you. Would you like that?'

Simon nodded and sniffed, and for a moment he gazed into Lorna's features. Then he turned away quickly and ran into the house. Lorna stared after him while tears came flooding to her eyes. Fearing that she would lose control of herself, and suspecting that Isobel was undoubtedly watching from a window, she turned quickly and got into the car.

She was unable to start the engine the first time. Her hands were trembling, her mind cluttered with emotion. Then she controlled herself ruthlessly and drove away. She left the estate and followed the narrow road that led into the mountains, trying not to break down as she drove forlornly, her back turned against her crumpling dreams.

Presently her tears overflowed and ran down her cheeks. Her lips quivered as misery washed through her. She pulled in at the side of the road and stopped the car, then subsided into a paroxysm of weeping. She sobbed unrestrainedly, filled with the bleak bitterness of despair.

By the time Lorna returned home she had to prepare for night duty, and she had managed to repair the ravages of her copious weeping. She had cried herself dry of tears and felt quite bereft of emotion as she entered the house. She was relieved that her parents were not in and hurriedly dressed in her uniform in order to be gone before she could be accosted by their return. When she checked her appearance in the dressing table mirror she found that make-up adequately covered the more obvious signs of her distress and, apart from a stiffness around her mouth and a hardness in her eyes, she seemed little different to normal.

She reached the hospital well before she was due to go on duty, and waited until it was time to slip into her routine. None of her personal thoughts intruded through the barrier she had set up in her mind, and when Jack Foster suddenly appeared in the doorway of the office while she was catching up on her reports she even managed a smile. But he gazed at her suspiciously, and it crossed her thoughts that he had seen Isobel recently and knew the latest developments in the situation. She could almost hear Isobel's gloating voice as she imagined the woman reporting that she had finally ended the opposition to their plans.

'Are you all right, Lorna,' Foster demanded.

'Certainly. Is there any reason why I shouldn't be?' Lorna shook her head and sighed. 'So you've learned that I've taken my leave of Simon. That means I shall not be seeing Julian again either. Perhaps Isobel has gained something from all of this, Jack, but I fail to see your advantage. You've been pressuring me, doing Isobel's dirty work for her. But you haven't helped yourself. You have gone down considerably in my estimation, even though you were motivated by the highest intentions.'

'You don't have to tell me,' he retorted moodily, and she judged that he had been drinking again. 'I've got the dirty end of the stick! I thought I was being very clever, seeing Isobel on the quiet, trying to find out what was happening between you and Kane. But tonight I found out that Isobel has merely been using me. I've been a fool. I realize that now it's too late. I never had much of a chance with you, Lorna, but what little there was is gone now.'

'You look as if you could do with some coffee,' she retorted. 'You'd better get some rest while you can. You've been getting away with a great deal lately, but it can't last. I'm sure Mr James knew you had been drinking before that emergency op. Don't be a fool and lose everything you've worked so hard for.'

He staggered slightly as he came across to the desk, but Lorna spoke again before he could say anything.

'Let us get some things straight, Jack. I have severed all links with the Kanes. I'll never see them again. Right now I just want to be left alone, and I don't want to hear their names mentioned or any talk of you and me. Just let it lie and let me forget everything.'

He stared at her, and she noted the faint smell of whisky permeating the atmosphere. She caught her breath, aware that he was taking no heed of her words, and frustration began to burn inside her. But she clamped down on it and returned to her work, ignoring his presence. After a moment of heavy silence he turned on his heel and stalked out of the office.

With her mind in such a heightened state, Lorna could only expect the night to prove troublesome. It was the last one of her tour of night duty, and she was hoping for an easy time. But from the start there were problems, and everything seemed to get out of hand. One of the nurses became ill and had to go off duty, and for two hours Lorna had to cope with the shortage until a relief nurse appeared. Then there were two emergencies for the operating Theatre, and she had to scrub to assist with one of them because of the staff shortage. The case was a private one, and Professor Taylor had been called. Jack Foster came to assist, and Lorna was appalled when he appeared, unsteady and still suffering from the effects of his drinking. But he was masked and gowned and stood across the table from the Professor, obviously trying to brace himself.

The operation was a success, but there was a crisis, and when the Professor suddenly cursed Foster for not holding a clamp tightly enough the Theatre filled with overpowering tension. The incident seemed to snatch away the last vestiges of Foster's under-mined self-confidence, and during the latter part of the operation Lorna was only too aware of the growing situation.

When the patient had been wheeled out of the Theatre the Professor turned on Foster. The two Theatre nurses were already busy cleaning up and Lorna was preparing to return to her work. She paused at the harsh voice as the Professor began to upbraid Foster, and despair settled into her mind, for there seemed no end to the repercussions arising from their personal lives.

'Foster, in all my years of experience I have never had to operate with a half-drunken assistant. I was told that you have been on duty in the past after a bout of drinking, and I could smell whisky across the table. I shall expect your resignation on my desk first thing in the morning, and you'd better not appear in the same Theatre with me again. If I ever set eyes on you in Theatre garb while I'm here then I'll have you charged with criminal negligence.'

The Professor stalked out of the Theatre and Lorna regarded the motionless Foster. He seemed turned to stone, and she felt a wave of sympathy for him. Going to his side, she touched his sleeve.

'Come along to my office, Jack, and I'll make some coffee,' she offered.

He jerked his arm free of her hand and

smiled thinly as he looked down into her eyes. 'Leave me alone. I've had just about as much as I can take. This is all I needed to round off what's been a perfect day, I don't think!'

He stalked away, and Lorna firmed her lips as she gazed after him with sinking spirits. She had the uncanny feeling that his actions would affect her in some way, although she could not even guess how. But she had her duties to attend to and there was no room in her mind for personal thoughts. She shrugged fatalistically and went back to the wards.

The rest of the night was like a bad dream. Time seemed to drag, and Lorna began to think the morning would never come. She suffered dreadfully as her thoughts plagued her, but bore it stoically, and when the Day Sister arrived to relieve her she felt as if a great weight had been lifted from her shoulders.

'Have a nice week-end,' her colleague said with a smile as Lorna departed.

Lorna smiled and shook her head, for there was no future to look forward to. In the normal course of events she would have been seeing Julian and Simon after a short sleep, but that pleasure was already a thing of the past. She went home, had a frugal breakfast, then went to bed, and slipped into a deep sleep after many trying minutes of forcing her mind to accept blankness. But sleep she did, and knew nothing more until a hand shook her awake and brought her back to reality.

'Lorna, wake up.' Mrs Parry was standing by the bed.

'What's the time?' Lorna stifled a yawn and sat up, frowning as she looked around and her thoughts returned. This was Saturday and she was off duty for two days.

'It's just past noon. Sorry to call you before you've had your full sleep, but I've had a telephone call from Cairn Manor and I felt that I had to call you, although you must still be dreadfully tired.'

'What's the trouble?' Lorna was fully

awake now, aroused by mention of the Manor.

'It's Simon. He can't be found anywhere. He and his pony are missing.'

Lorna was out of bed in a flash and reaching for her dressing gown. 'I'll get dressed,' she said. 'I'd better get out there right away.'

'Julian said perhaps Simon came looking for you, so would we search around here and make enquiries at the hospital. Perhaps the boy thinks you're on duty.'

Lorna's mind was beginning to work normally now, although she was cold with shock. It was obvious that her parting from Simon had hit the boy harder than she had imagined, or else Isobel had upset him again.

'While I'm dressing perhaps you'd ring the hospital and put them on the alert. How long has he been missing?'

'Since early this morning. He went out after breakfast to look at the pony, so Julian said, but the chauffeur failed to find him anywhere in the vicinity, and he's never left the paddock before.'

Lorna prepared to set out, her mind filled with fresh worry. Her own problems were thrust into the background, and she pictured Simon's face as she wondered what might have happened at the Manor. The boy had been bitterly upset the day before, and that might be the key to his disappearance.

When she went down to the hall Mrs Parry was using the phone, and Lorna waited in a foment of apprehension. Mrs Parry put down the receiver and turned slowly, a grave expression upon her face.

'Simon hasn't been seen around the hospital,' she reported. 'They're going to watch for him. Where can you search, Lorna?'

'I don't know.' Lorna was completely at a loss. She was still tired, and there was reproach in her mind for the way she had handled yesterday's situation. She realized now that she ought not to have given in to

Isobel so easily. But she had thought at the time it would be better for Simon.

'You don't think he's fallen into the pool again, do you?' Mrs Parry demanded.

'Mother, don't put thoughts like that into my mind.' Lorna scarcely dared think of the possibilities. 'I'd better drive out to the Manor. Simon wouldn't willingly run away, and there's the pony. I suspect he's gone for a ride over the moors.'

'But surely he hasn't got permission to do something like that!' Mrs Parry stared at her in disbelief. 'Those moors are dangerous.'

'You don't have to tell me.' Lorna was impatient to leave. 'He wouldn't be permitted to ride out there alone. It's possible that he decided to do so.'

'What's happened to cause all this upset?' Her mother looked at Lorna with narrowed eyes.

'There's no time to tell you now, but there was some trouble yesterday that could be at the back of all this. Stay here, Mother, in case anyone telephones, and I'll keep in touch with you.'

She hurried from the house and fetched the car from the garage, then drove out to the Manor as fast as she dared. When she arrived she saw the chauffeur and Isobel Garvin by the pool, and the man was apparently dragging the pool. Lorna parked her car and hurried across to them, her mind teetering under the shock of what was happening.

'Hasn't he been found yet?' Lorna demanded.

'No.' Isobel stared at her with cold blue eyes. 'Hasn't he turned up at your place?'

'I haven't set eyes upon him. Where's Julian?'

'Out looking for him, where else?' Isobel spoke in sullen tones. 'This is what comes of giving the boy too much freedom.'

'Has the entire estate been searched?' interrupted Lorna. 'Does he have any favourite places where he's likely to go? Is it possible that he's gone riding, stopped somewhere and fallen asleep?'

'There's no sign of the pony, so he's gone right away from the estate,' said the chauffeur. 'I've looked everywhere, and Mr Kane has gone farther afield, although the boy shouldn't have wandered off the estate.'

Lorna gazed down into the murky water of the pool and recalled the morning when she had dived in to save Simon's life. She sighed as she turned away and went back to her car, ignoring Isobel. She drove on to the house, and as she drew up at the bottom of the steps Mrs Heywood appeared in the doorway.

'I'm glad you've arrived,' said the housekeeper. She looked as if she'd been crying. 'There was a telephone call for you a few minutes ago. It was a Mr Foster. He said he knew you were on your way here. Would you ring him back at the hospital?'

'Thank you. Is Mr Kane around?'

'He's out looking for Simon. Don't you have any idea where he might be, Sister?'

'I wish I did. What was his manner this morning?'

261

'He seemed all right at breakfast. It was a real upset he had yesterday. But he seemed eager to get out to his pony. The men of the estate are out searching now. They have the pony to look for as well. It's possible that Simon had an accident, isn't it?'

'Quite possible. That's why he was warned never to leave the paddock, and I can't believe that he would willingly do so.' Lorna frowned as she tried to think over the possibilities. 'Have the police been informed?' There was a tremor in her voice as she asked the question.

'Not yet. Mr Kane thinks he must be somewhere close to the estate. Heaven forbid that they should have to be called in.'

Lorna followed the housekeeper into the house and went to the telephone. She called the hospital and asked for Jack Foster. A few moments later his voice sounded in her ear.

'It's Lorna,' she said.

'Has the child been found yet?' he demanded harshly.

'No. Everyone is out looking. What do you want, Jack?'

'I need to talk to you, and as soon as possible.'

'It can't be anything more urgent than finding Simon.' Lorna compressed her lips.

'If you come and talk with me the chances are that you'll locate him,' Foster said slowly.

'What do you mean?' A pang of fear seemed to squeeze Lorna's heart.

'I mean that possibly it was arranged for him to have an accident on his pony. The animal is missing with him, isn't it?'

'You're joking!' Lorna caught her breath, and blood pounded at her temples. She lifted a hand to her mouth as a stream of terrifying pictures poured through her mind, activated by his words.

'Joking is the last thing I feel like,' he responded curtly. 'Since I heard that he'd gone missing I've been putting two and two together. Now I've got to talk to you, and don't let anyone there know what I've said.

Meet me immediately. I've been suspended from duty. I'll be waiting in my car near your home.'

'I'm on my way back now,' she said instantly, and frowned as she replaced the receiver. She turned to the waiting house-keeper. 'Tell Julian I called, won't you? I'll ring again soon. But this may be important.'

'Has it anything to do with Simon?' Mrs Heywood demanded, and Lorna hesitated for a moment before shaking her head.

She went out to her car, and as she was driving away from the house she had to pull over for Julian's car coming towards her. She stopped and alighted, and he got out of his car and approached quickly, his face showing great strain.

'Any signs of him?' she asked breathlessly.

'I was about to ask you the same thing.' He spoke in a clipped way, and there was fear in his tone. 'What do you think happened to him, Lorna? I've been along the road across the moors but didn't see anything. Why would he go off like this?'

'Have you informed the police yet of his disappearance?' she countered.

'No. I'm afraid to take that step.'

'They're better equipped to make a search.'

'I'll ring them when I get to the house.' He gazed into her face and she felt her heart go out to him at the sight of the raw fear in his eyes. But he seemed almost like a stranger and she wondered what had happened to the situation that had grown up around them. Everything seemed finished, dead and already decaying.

'He was rather upset yesterday when I called,' she said slowly, aware that this was not the time to discuss events. But she could not permit him to believe only Isobel's side of the situation.

'You were out here yesterday?' Surprise showed in his face. 'I didn't know. I wasn't told. But I didn't get in until very late last night, and when I arose this morning I was met with this nightmare.'

Out of the corner of her eye Lorna could

see Isobel and the chauffeur approaching, and she moved impatiently.

'I have to be going now,' she said. 'I'll check with you again later, Julian. I'm going to keep looking myself, but we won't find him standing around here.'

'You're right, but I don't know where to look next. I'm going to leave the car and take a horse to cross the moors. I'll have to try and track him down, that's all.'

Lorna nodded and turned away, hurrying to her car, and her mind was filled with sorrow beneath the wedge of concern for Simon which lay in its upper reaches. She drove back to town, her thoughts sombre, her eyes narrowed against the sunlight. She did not know which way to turn next, but something had to be done, and that was the only firm fact available.

When she turned into the road where her house was situated she saw Jack Foster's car parked at the kerb in front, and pulled in behind him, alighting to go to his car. He was watching her and opened the nearside door. His face was set in grim lines, his eyes bleary, as she looked at him.

'Well?' she demanded immediately. 'What about Simon? Why the telephone call, and what did it mean?' She got into the car at his side, wondering if he had been drinking again, and the smell of whisky tugged at her nostrils. Impatience filled her, but she fought it down. Simon was missing, and nothing mattered but that the boy was found quickly and in good health.

'Lorna, I don't know quite how to put this,' Foster said slowly. 'What happened to me at the hospital last night seems to have brought me to my senses, made my thoughts slip into focus. I've been playing a foolish game and I must have been crazy to think it would work. I was crazy! Crazy in love with you. But I can see now that I never had a chance with you, and what I have done in my attempts to make you love me has only made my behaviour worse.'

'What are you getting at, Jack? You said something about an accident being arranged for Simon. For Heaven's sake, if this isn't just another ruse of yours then tell me all about it so we can do something. We have to concentrate all our efforts on locating that boy. If you do have anything to tell me that may help find him then get to the point.' She stared into his face but he could not meet her gaze.

'I can drive you to the spot where I think the boy will be, with his pony, and there's likely to be no real threat against him until night has fallen. But I want to play down the events leading up to this.'

'Why? Because you've been involved? Look, start driving, for Heaven's sake. Talk to me as we make progress.'

He started the car and pulled away from the kerb so violently that Lorna was thrown back in her seat. She clenched her teeth and fastened her seat belt. He had been drinking again, and seemed almost incapable of driving. But her fears for Simon outweighed any concern for her own safety.

'What kind of a mess have you got yourself

into?' she demanded.

'I struck a bargain with Isobel,' he said hesitantly, gazing ahead. 'We would do whatever was necessary to part you and Kane. I saw Kane and told him that before he stuck his nose into your life you and I were on the point of becoming engaged. That's why he's changed his attitude towards you. He's acting in the gentlemanly way! He's dropping out of your life so you can find happiness with me.'

'But you know that I'll never turn to you!' Lorna cried.

'I do, now. But I suspect that Isobel knew it all the time, and was just using me for her own ends. But when I realized that I had lost you I'd gone too far to back out. Now I've lost my position at the hospital and ruined my life, but not only mine; I've ruined yours as well.'

'What about Simon?' Lorna demanded, feeling a sense of urgency creeping into her mind. 'You say there's no danger to him until tonight?'

'The moors are dangerous, especially after dark, and that boy will be wandering around alone out there all day. When it does get dark he'll panic and must surely fall into a pothole or a bog. He could disappear without trace.'

'But why has he gone out there? And where is he?'

'Isobel has more at stake in this than I. No one has to tell me that I've lost. But I didn't realize just how far she would go to get what she wants. The trouble is, Simon hates her, and she knows there's little chance of succeeding with Julian Kane while the boy is alive. Kane never had much time for the lad until he almost drowned. That brought it home to him, and Isobel has been fighting a losing battle since you became the heroine. But she never told me her plans. She's too deep-natured to commit herself. But I've been putting two and two together and they add up to a very frightening four, especially when I heard that Simon had gone missing.'

Lorna gazed intently at him, wondering if

he was telling the truth. He was driving fast towards the town limits, and she was scared by the way he handled the car.

'Where are you taking me, Jack?' she demanded.

'When I've been out with Isobel we've driven across the moors, and several times we've visited a cottage that's off the beaten track, right on the edge of Kane's estate. Several comments she's made out there makes me suspect that she's planned to send the boy riding out that way, to wait for you. She's used you as bait. The boy would go to the ends of the earth to see you, especially after you said goodbye to him last night. When it gets dark Isobel is going out to the cottage and plans to leave the boy somewhere to die of exposure. It sounds melodramatic, doesn't it? But it just shows how determined Isobel is. She'll stop at nothing to get what she wants. But she under-estimated me. She thought I would go as far to get you as she was prepared to go to get Kane. But I'm afraid I'm not that

271

strong a character. Thank Heaven I did learn enough of her intentions to piece it all together.'

'But you've let this advance to a late stage, haven't you?' demanded Lorna, horrified by the thought of Simon being out on the moors alone. 'Can't you realize how much of a shock this will give Simon?'

'I didn't let it go this far knowingly,' he retorted sourly. He concentrated upon his driving as they followed a narrow, twisting road. 'Isobel was throwing out hints for some time, and no doubt she was testing me, trying to find out just how far I would go. Well I suppose yesterday was a turning point in her life, for you withdrew from the Kane family circle. She told me last night that our efforts had failed and she was giving up the whole affair. I believed her, until I heard this morning that the boy was missing. It is possible that this is just a coincidence, but I wouldn't like to bet on it.'

'But surely she must know she's taking a big risk by letting this happen after letting you in on so much of it!' Lorna still had doubts about his story, and began to wonder if he was merely spinning a fantastic yarn in order to get her out on the moors alone.

'Simon is due to die of exposure. It would be an accident. No one could be blamed.'

'Hurry up and get to the cottage,' Lorna directed. 'We've got to get there as quickly as possible.'

'Hold tight then!' The car surged forward as he pressed his foot down on the accelerator.

Lorna's thoughts teemed through her mind, and they seemed so unreal. But when she considered Isobel she realized that the secretary did have a calculating streak in her, and after witnessing the incident with the pony, Lorna found it easy to accept that Isobel could go to the lengths Foster predicted. She bit her lip as the car sped on. She knew where the remote cottage was, and was aware of the dangers in the situation. Anything could happen to Simon even in daylight.

Foster sent the big car dashing along the narrow roads, and Lorna kept glancing at his harshly set features. His knuckles were white as he gripped the steering wheel and there was a determined glint in his eyes which seemed to promise that he was going to do all he could to help find the missing boy. He glanced at her once after the car had skidded slightly on a bend that proved to be more acute than it looked.

'Is your safety belt fixed correctly?' he demanded. 'This road is too narrow for comfort.'

She checked the belt, then noticed that he was not wearing his. When she remonstrated with him he nodded, and smiled tightly.

'I haven't the time to stop. It isn't too far now, thank the Lord!' The car was speeding up a hill and Lorna tensed in her seat, thrown against the restraining belt as they took a bend in dangerous fashion.

'Perhaps you'd better slow down a little,' she suggested.

'I know the road quite well,' he retorted.

The next instant they were almost flying over the crest of a hill, and Lorna cried a warning as she sensed that the car was losing its hold upon the road. She instinctively braced herself, her eyes widening as she glanced at Foster and saw him fighting the wheel. But the car suddenly slewed sideways and the next instant they were leaving the road and crashing through a low stone wall. Lorna barely had time to throw up her hands to protect her face before the windscreen shattered. Then the car lurched wildly and turned over. The whole world seemed to whirl about them, to the accompaniment of fearsome sounds as metal slammed against rock and protested with ear-splitting intensity. The next instant Lorna received a hard blow on the side of her head, and all sight and sound vanished as a black peacefulness enveloped her.

TWELVE

Returning to consciousness seemed like a nightmare to Lorna. She was at first dimly aware of pain in her body but could not pinpoint it. Then her mind began to return to harsh reality and her first animated thought was that she might be late for duty. Slowly her eyes opened, and she discovered that her pains came from the restraining seat belt cutting across her body and waist. She blinked, wondering dully why she was in such a peculiar position, and then recognised her surroundings as Jack Foster's car, and it was lying on its offside. She gasped as her memory returned slowly.

Groaning a little, she looked around, wondering what had become of Jack. She was badly shocked and her thoughts were stilted, not flowing in their usual quicksilver fashion. When she looked at her hands she saw blood dribbling from a bad cut on the back of her right hand. She stared at the blood for some moments, and the sight of it slowly cleared her mind. She instinctively checked the rest of her body, and, apart from a tender area on the left side of her head just above the temple, she seemed to be all right. But she was surprised that no bones were broken and her only injury seemed to be the cut hand.

She swung her feet around until she was standing on the driver's door, then released herself from the seat belt. She was aware that the belt had undoubtedly saved her from much worse injuries and probably saved her life, and then she recalled that Jack had not been wearing his belt and she scrambled hastily out of the car by way of the gaping space where the windscreen had been.

She found herself standing unsteadily at the bottom of a slope, and there was a trail of glass and torn-up earth along the slope, leading back up to the hole in the wall where they had left the road. She looked around anxiously for Jack, believing that he had probably gone for help, and then she saw his inert figure lying in a clump of gorse. She staggered across to him, dropping to her knees at his side, and a sob escaped her when she saw that he was dead.

He must have been thrown through the windscreen! He died instantly, she decided. His head and shoulders were covered with blood and a piece of glass had pierced his jugular.

She wept as she pushed herself to her feet and looked around at the empty landscape. Drops of blood were falling copiously from her hand and she went back to the car and reached into the glove compartment for the first aid tin she knew Foster always carried. Sitting down on the grass, she attended to her injury, stopping the bleeding, treating the wound efficiently and bandaging it.

When she climbed the slope to the hole in the wall and regained the road, Lorna gazed around dazedly. Her head was aching intolerably and she was having difficulty in collecting her wits. She gazed along the dusty road, wondering where she had been going in the car with Jack. Then it all came back to her and she drew a deep breath, holding it for long moments as she fought to control the hysteria that threatened to overwhelm her. The facts began to tumble into her mind. Simon was missing. Jack had been taking her to the remote cottage, where the boy might be.

She looked at the wrecked car, at Foster's immobile figure lying in the gorse, and then turned and started walking along the road, making towards the distant cottage which lay along a diverging track, her feet dragging. She wanted to get to a telephone, but the urgency was strangely remote in her mind, and only a picture of Simon's face kept her going when every inclination was to drop to the ground and rest.

She seemed to be stranded in an uncanny limbo, and Lorna had no idea how long or how far she walked. She knew the area well, and was aware of the location of the cottage, but she didn't seem to be making any progress in the hot afternoon. She staggered and reeled, falling several times, until she topped a mound and saw the little cottage sweltering in the heat.

The sound of a car alerted her, dragged her thoughts back to alertness, and she looked ahead to see a car coming towards her, leaving a slight dust haze behind. It halted beside her, and a woman's face peered intently at her.

'Have you been involved in an accident?'

Lorna smiled faintly, leaning unsteadily against the car. The question struck her as being incongruous, but she fought against encroaching weakness and nodded, quickly explaining what had occurred.

'Get in and I'll drive you into Rossglen.' the woman said.

'No. I have something else to do. But please report the accident to the police, and make a telephone call to Julian Kane at

Cairn Manor. Tell him Lorna Parry sent the message, and would he come to the crofter's cottage on the edge of his estate. That's the one, over there.' Lorna pointed to the building in the distance.

'Are you sure you're not suffering from shock?' demanded the woman. 'I'm sure it would be better for you to come with me.'

'No. Appearances are not what they seem. If you'll do what I ask then everything will be all right.'

The woman gazed at Lorna for a moment, then came to a decision and drove on. Lorna gazed after the car, sighing heavily, trying to maintain her alertness. But her head ached and she felt an increasing desire to lie down and rest. She looked at the cottage and forced herself to go on.

The cottage was deserted. No one had lived in it for years, and it was badly overgrown. Lorna paused by the dilapidated garden fence and fought against tears. There was no sign of Simon. She had expected to see him waiting here for her.

Had Jack been lying after all? She sank down upon a rock and let her shoulders slump. She was tired, and shock was numbing her thoughts. But she needed to find Simon, and pushed herself up and began to look for signs of a pony's passing. It was likely that Simon had tired of waiting and returned to the Manor. But she could not accept that. Now she was here she would have to make a thorough search.

How long she staggered around she could not afterwards recall, for shock and concussion blurred her senses. When she heard a youthful voice calling to her she paused and looked around, ready to disbelieve all evidence, including her sight, but there was Simon on his pony, riding towards her, his face wreathed in smiles. Lorna was so relieved at seeing him that she sank to the ground, and he came up to her and slid out of the saddle to hurry to her side.

'Lorna, I'm so pleased to see you. When I got here and didn't find you I thought you hadn't waited. I've been riding round and round because I thought you'd come. You wouldn't change your mind.' His chatter trailed off as he looked at her, and then his words were higher pitched. 'What's wrong, Lorna? You're covered in blood. You've hurt yourself.'

Lorna sighed and pushed herself to her feet, and Simon looked at her bandaged hand. Blood was seeping through the white material, and Lorna glanced at it, then began to comfort him, for his face had paled.

'It's all right, Simon. Look, we'd better go back to the cottage. I asked your father to find us there, and he won't take long in coming. But why were you out here all alone? You've been told not to leave the paddock.'

The boy confirmed Jack Foster's story as they set off back to the cottage. Isobel had told him that Lorna would be arriving at the cottage, and sent him to the rendezvous, warning him to wait there until Lorna showed. He was now tired and hungry, but happy because Lorna had arrived.

When they reached the cottage Simon spotted a car coming along a track which crossed the moors from the direction of Cairn Manor, and a few moments later Julian and his chauffeur were alighting. Lorna felt her legs lose their strength as Julian reached her, and he put an arm around her. For a few moments there was confusion as their several voices sounded, but Julian could see that Lorna was exhausted, and made her sit down.

'Now tell me all about this,' he said. 'I had a telephone call from the police, passing on a message from a woman who had reported a fatal accident. We broke all records getting here, and the police asked us to wait until they arrive. You look as if you're going to pay a visit to the hospital, Lorna. But can you tell me exactly what has been going on?'

'Jack Foster is dead.' Her tone sounded hollow when she spoke, and she could hardly believe the fact as she heard her own voice relaying the information. Julian's face hardened as he listened to her account, and when she lapsed into silence he put his arms around her.

'Lorna, will you ever be able to forgive me?' he demanded. 'I cooled off towards you because Foster spoke to me, told me that he and you were on the point of becoming engaged when I turned up. I didn't want to spoil your chances. But this business with Isobel sounds incredible. She's been my secretary for a long time. I didn't know she had secret ambitions to be my wife, and at the expense of Simon's life.' He glanced across to where the boy was standing with the chauffeur, patting the pony. 'There has been some trouble over the past few days. Mrs Heywood was telling me something about it when I got your message to come here. But she didn't know much. She explained about Simon giving her trouble and you soothing him. But something happened yesterday while I was away, didn't it?'

'There's so much to tell,' Lorna said

quietly, thinking of Jack Foster. He had atoned for all the trouble he had caused. He lost his life trying to help save Simon.

'Most of it can wait,' Julian cut in. 'You're in shock, Lorna, and I don't need to be a medical practitioner to see that. All that matters is that we've found Simon and that you haven't changed your attitude towards us. I found it difficult to believe when it was told to me, but I wouldn't cause you any disquiet by demanding an explanation. Simon and I are in your debt as it is. But Isobel has a lot to answer for. My wife lost her life on the moors, and it's been a mystery ever since why she went out there. Perhaps Isobel knows the answer. I expect the police will have some questions to ask her when they can get around to it. But she knows about the message for me to come here. She was in the hall when I received it, and I repeated it. I couldn't understand it at the time, and when I did mention it she seemed rather perturbed, although I attributed her reaction to quite different reasons. I think we're going to be lucky to find her at the Manor when we return.'

Lorna leaned her head against his comforting shoulder and closed her eyes. She felt dizzy, and her head ached intolerably.

'Come on.' Julian arose, then picked her up effortlessly and carried her towards the car. 'I'm taking you to the Manor and the police can come there to talk to you. Hopkins.' He called to the chauffeur. 'Stay here and inform the police that I've taken Sister Parry to the Manor. Wait with the pony and I'll send one of the men with the horse box. Simon is going back with us. I'm not letting him out of my sight after this.'

'I'll start walking back with the pony, Mr Kane,' the chauffeur said, 'after the police have been.'

Lorna closed her eyes as Julian put her on the back seat, and Simon sat beside her, holding her arm.

'Are you sure you shouldn't go to the hospital for attention to that hand?' Julian demanded anxiously. 'It looks as if it's bleeding badly, Lorna.'

'It will be all right. Perhaps it should have a stitch in it, but I'd rather not go there now. I couldn't face my colleagues now Jack is dead.'

'What happened on the road wasn't your fault,' he reminded, getting into the car.' 'Don't reproach yourself for it. Foster seemed a bad sort, but he came good in the end, and I'm sorry it had to cost him his life. It's just something else that must rest on Isobel's shoulders.'

He drove on, and there was blessed silence until they reached the Manor. Lorna and Simon walked into the big house while Julian went on ahead, but when they reached the hall Mrs Heywood was explaining that Isobel had packed a bag and left hurriedly. The housekeeper's voice was the last thing Lorna heard. A wave of stifling blackness seemed to spring up about her and she fell heavily to the ground.

When she came to her senses once more she was in bed in a large room, and her father was standing at the foot of the bed, with Julian at his side. They were silent, and had evidently been there quite some time. At her movement, her father came forward, and he smiled encouragingly as he bent over her.

'Lorna,' he said softly. 'How are you feeling now?'

She sighed, aware of Julian's presence. Then she nodded slowly. Her head did not ache so much, but she felt exhausted.

'I'm much better,' she replied. 'What's the time?'

'Seven in the evening.'

'You'll stay here overnight,' said Julian, coming forward. 'You need the rest. Simon's room is next door.'

'I'll give you a sedative, something to ensure that you get a good night's sleep,' her father said.

'No thank you, Father. I'd rather not. I'm not feeling too badly now.'

'All right. I have to go now. But Julian can call if you need me. You've had a harrowing experience so get plenty of rest. Mother wants me to telephone and let her know how you are. We're all thankful that you came out of this so lightly. I'll come in tomorrow morning to see you.'

He bent and kissed her forehead, then departed, and Julian saw him out, to return moments later, followed by a uniformed policeman.

'I'm sorry to trouble you, Miss,' the policeman told her, 'but I must get a statement from you, if you're feeling up to it.'

Lorna nodded, aware that this was an ordeal she would be grateful to put behind her. Julian sat beside the bed, lightly holding her hand while she narrated the events that had taken place. Then the constable departed, informing her that she would have to talk again to others, but for the moment she would be left alone.

Julian bent over her, kissing her gently on the lips. His dark eyes were moist, gleaming, and Lorna drew a long, deep breath and held it.

'It must seem like a nightmare to you,' he whispered. 'I'm sure it's been one of the worst days I've ever experienced. But Simon and I want you to know that you're the most important person in the world as far as we're concerned, Lorna.'

'Where is Simon?' she asked. 'And what about Isobel?'

'I've decided that nothing should be said to the police about Isobel,' Julian told her quietly. 'I don't want a scandal, Lorna. I think it would be better for Simon if nothing of this came out. If you think otherwise, then, of course, I'll take the necessary steps. But that is up to you.'

Lorna thought of Jack Foster, and knew there would be a stigma attached to his memory if the whole truth came out. She shook her head.

'No, Julian. Let it rest there. Isobel has gone and that's the main thing. Now let me see Simon. At one time I began to think I would never see his face again.'

Julian smiled and went to the door, and a

subdued Simon entered the room to come and stand beside the bed. Lorna held out a hand to him and he clasped it tightly.

'I'm so glad you're not going to take that other job, Lorna,' he said. 'Daddy told me you're going to stay here with us. I told you I wanted you to come and live in the Manor with us, didn't I?'

Lorna nodded, then looked at Julian, who was also nodding, and she knew the nightmare was ending. But Julian came forward.

'No more talking now,' he commanded in his masterful way. 'I think you should follow the doctor's orders, Lorna, and get some rest. Simon will he going to bed presently, in the next room, and we'll talk more in the morning, when I hope you'll be completely recovered. Say goodnight, Simon, and we'll leave Lorna to sleep.'

They departed, Simon leaving reluctantly, and Lorna sank back into the comfortable bed and closed her eyes. There was a shadow overhanging the joy in her mind, and that was caused by the death of Jack

Foster. But time would take care of that, she knew from bitter experience, and the future seemed to be set fair. She lapsed into slumber without being aware of the fact, and the next time she opened her eyes the room was dark.

She lay for a moment trying to collect herself, and hazy memories flitted across her mind. Then she came to full awareness, for there was the acrid tang of smoke in the room. She frowned, ready to believe that she was dreaming, but her throat was raspy and she threw aside the bedcovers and pulled on her dressing gown, which lay across the foot of the bed. When she hurried to the door she turned the handle and pulled, but the door would not budge, and she wrestled with the handle for several moments before accepting the fact that it was locked.

The smoke seemed to be filtering up through the floorboards, and she fancied she could feel heat under the soles of her feet. Dropping to her hands and knees, she began to cough as smoke entered her lungs.

Her mind was half drugged with slumber and shock, but the smoke cut through the fog and she realized that the house was on fire.

Hammering at the door with her clenched hands, she shouted for help, Simon was asleep in the next room, but she had no idea where Julian's bedroom was. She paused and listened intently for some response to her alarm, but there was nothing. Again she tried the door handle, and wondered why the door should be locked.

Full alertness returned to her mind and she went quickly to the window, throwing it wide, and smoke seemed to be swirling up from below. When she peered out into the starry night she looked down and saw a red glow emanating from a ground floor room. Horror filled her. The fire had taken hold and was spreading rapidly, yet no one was aware of the fact.

She glanced to the left towards the window of Simon's room. There was no light on there and no sound from within.

When she saw the thick creeper on the wall she did not hesitate, but climbed out over the sill, although she had no head for heights, and began to work her way to the next window.

The creeper was strong, and she found easy hand and footholds, but several times her weight pulled the clinging vegetation away from the wall and she feared that she would plunge to the stone terrace below. When she paused for breath she looked down again, and saw quite clearly the ominous red glow of the spreading fire. But what she could not understand was why there was no reaction from Julian.

Heat was already rising outside by the time she reached the window of Simon's room, and she was relieved to discover a small window unfastened which enabled her to reach in and open a larger one. When she slid breathlessly into the room she found Simon still restlessly asleep in his bed. When she awakened him he gasped and then clung to her, but Lorna could not afford to waste any time. She went to the door, and clenched her teeth when she discovered it was also locked, and there was no key on the inside. They had both been locked in.

'Simon!' She turned resolutely to him. 'Listen to me and don't be afraid. The house is on fire and we can't get out of our rooms. The only way out is to climb down the creeper to the terrace. Do you think you can do that?'

'I'm frightened, Lorna,' he said instantly. 'Where's Daddy?'

'I don't know, and that's why we must hurry. Come along. We have to get over the sill and climb down. I'll go first, and I'll be with you all the time. Just remember to hold firmly to the creeper and don't look down. Put your shoes on.'

She spoke calmly, although her mind was steeped in fear. But she was afraid for Simon, not herself, and could only wonder about Julian. She edged out to the creeper again, and her heart seemed to be in her mouth as she waited for Simon to pluck up enough courage to join her. His face was shadowed, but he slid over the sill and let her guide his feet to thicker stems of creeper. She covered him with her body so that he could not see the ground and she would be able to grasp him should he lose his grip. They had to work thcir way to the right to get clear of the rising smoke and flames from the burning room.

It seemed a lifetime before they reached ground level, but the sound of the fire urged them on, and Lorna almost collapsed in relief when she finally touched foot upon the terrace and grasped Simon bodily to run to safety. It was not until they were clear of the terrace that she felt reaction begin to grip her, and her knees trembled as she looked towards the house and saw that the drawing room was burning furiously.

'Where's Daddy?' Simon demanded, and the sound of his voice broke the shock which held Lorna paralysed. She grasped his hand and they ran around to the front of the house.

When she rang the doorbell there was no reply, and she asked Simon which room Julian occupied. When the boy pointed it out, Lorna found a stone and shattered the bedroom window. A moment later Julian's head appeared.

'The house is on fire!' Lorna shouted.

Julian's head was withdrawn immediately, and Lorna led Simon back to the front door. She felt a sense of unreality gripping her as they waited, but a sound on the gravelled drive alerted her and she turned quickly to see two figures coming towards the house. One was a uniformed policeman, and he was grasping the second figure. At that moment the front door was opened and Mrs Heywood emerged from the house in a hurry.

'Sister Parry, how did you and Simon get out?' the housekeeper demanded.

'Where is Julian?' countered Lorna anxiously.

'Phoning the fire brigade.'

Julian appeared then, wrapped in a dressing gown, and as he reached Lorna and Simon and put his hands upon their shoulders the policeman arrived.

'Your secretary,' he said, thrusting Isobel forward. 'I caught her sneaking out of the grounds. May I use the phone? I want a car to take her to the station.'

'You'll have to hurry,' replied Julian calmly. 'The house is burning. I've phoned the brigade, but there's nothing we can do, the blaze is too fierce. But perhaps Isobel can tell us how it started.'

'Before she says anything, I want to tell you that my bedroom door was locked on the outside, and so was Simon's,' Lorna cut in. She explained how she and Simon had escaped from the fire.

'Would you really go to those lengths?' Julian demanded, gazing in disbelief at Isobel.

'Time for questions later,' the policeman said firmly, and took Isobel with him into the house.

Julian pulled Lorna closer into his embrace and looked down into her shadowed features. She in turn hugged Simon to her side.

'You've done it again, haven't you?' he demanded softly. 'I don't know how Isobel managed to get into the house, but we could have been burned in our beds. Don't ever leave us, Lorna, because I don't know how Simon and I would ever manage without you. In fact, I wonder how we ever got along before we knew you.'

Lorna let her head fall against his shoulder and her lips touched his cheek. She closed her eyes and let her mind go blank. Words were not necessary now. She had a family again; two people who really needed her, and when the unpleasantness was over there was no doubt that life would become very good. She felt Simon's chubby hand clasp her own, and all the aches and pains in her body seemed to ease as love flowed through her. Then Julian kissed her gently, and his action set the seal upon her dreams. She felt the last vestiges of her tragic past shrivel into insignificance as her mind became swamped with the promise of the future. She could even feel sorry for Isobel as the policeman brought her out of the house. The woman had acted through love, and love was everything.

The publishers hope that this book has given you enjoyable reading. Large Print Books are especially designed to be as easy to see and hold as possible. If you wish a complete list of our books please ask at your local library or write directly to:

Dales Large Print Books
Magna House, Long Preston,
Skipton, North Yorkshire.
BD23 4ND

This Large Print Book for the partially sighted, who cannot read normal print, is published under the auspices of
THE ULVERSCROFT FOUNDATION